Love Child
Penguin Books

Jean Bedford was born in Cambridge, England in 1946 and came to Australia in 1947. She was brought up in Victoria and after university taught English as a second language and worked as a journalist. She was Literary Editor of the *National Times* and now works as a literary consultant. In 1982 she won the Stanford Writing Fellowship and travelled to the United States to take it up. Jean Bedford's short stories have appeared in *Nation Review*, the *National Times* and *Meanjin*, and a collection of her short stories, *Country Girl Again*, was published in 1979; her novel, *Sister Kate*, was published in 1982.

Jean Bedford lives in Sydney and has three daughters.

Other books by Jean Bedford

Country Girl Again   (1979)
Sister Kate   (1982)

LOVE CHILD

JEAN BEDFORD

PENGUIN BOOKS

Penguin Books Australia Ltd,
487 Maroondah Highway, P.O. Box 257
Ringwood, Victoria 3134, Australia
Penguin Books Ltd,
Harmondsworth, Middlesex, England
Penguin Books,
40 West 23rd Street, New York, N.Y. 10010, U.S.A.
Penguin Books Canada Limited,
2801 John Street, Markham, Ontario, Canada L3R 1B4
Penguin Books (N.Z.) Ltd,
182-190 Wairau Road, Auckland 10, New Zealand

First published by Penguin Books Australia, 1986

Typeset in Paladium by Midland Typesetters Pty Ltd, Maryborough
Made and printed in Australia by
The Dominion Press-Hedges & Bell, Maryborough

CIP

Bedford, Jean, 1946-
Love child.

ISBN 0 14 008465 7.

I. Title.
A823'.3

A section of this novel was published in the *National Times*
in a slightly different form, as a short story called 'Mistletoe'.

For Gabrielle Lord

ACKNOWLEDGEMENTS

This novel was written with the assistance of: the 1982/83 Stanford Australian Writers Fellowship; the 1983 NSW Premier's Literary Grant; and a General Writers Grant from the Literature Board of the Australia Council. I acknowledge this assistance with gratitude.

There's never much to read
Between the lines of what we need
And what we'll take.
. . . Between the lines of photographs
I've seen the past,
It isn't pleasing.'

Janis Ian

1

The girls grew up in a slum, a tenement in London.
There were five of them and Grace was the oldest. They
had three rooms in their flat, and the use of the
bathroom on the floor below. But to get to it you had
to pass Boney, and if you forgot to salute he would
catch you in his crabbed fingers there in the dim passage
with its smell of other people's stale cooking, and
threaten in his phoney French wheeze. The child Grace
found it easy to believe he might be Napoleon. She had
seen through a crack in his door how he lined up his
wife and children shivering naked to inspect the ranks.

Stranger things happened. Her own father beat the
girls when he was drunk, with his spare wooden arm.
Grace would laugh, later, telling her daughter, her
friends, about it, but it wasn't funny at the time. (The
fingers hurt most, cruel and stiff, though the back of
the wooden hand could still bruise.)

From as long as she could remember there was
always a new baby for her to look after. She fidgeted
uneasily through her lessons at the Dame school,
hoping Mrs Rattray down the hall had not forgotten
again to wash the nappies. She ran home up the steep
cobbles, always anxious about what she might find.
Wondering if she would have the time before her father

1

got home to tidy up, get the vegetables simmering, everything ready for her tired mother coming back from the factory so that he wouldn't shout and threaten. If they could keep him in a good mood he might take their mother with him when he went to the pub, for a stout, and Grace would push the baby in its pram and herd the toddlers to the iron-gated park, and perhaps there would be a penny for some fried potatoes. And then perhaps he would not get too drunk and the spare arm would stay in its cardboard box under the big bed.

But if the nappies were not washed, and if Grace had to do that, first, because the smell of dirty nappies was sure to set him off, then there might not be time to clean the small room, put away the rattles and the wooden doll, three times broken and mended after his rage; there might not be time to wash the dishes and set the table, find the penny for the gas, prepare the vegetables and put them in their pot, before he stalked in, his face clenched and suspicious, his blue eyes twinkling meanly, his gloved, useless arm stiff at his side as he searched every shabby corner in one sweeping glance from wall to wall. Then it would be all useless, she knew. Useless the trembling haste to help him off with his coat, find his slippers, put the steaming strong tea by his chair. Because he would be watching as she tried to quietly, oh quietly, finish things. Her hands would shake, she might cut herself feeling his stare at the thickness of her peelings, the knife itself useless and limp in her fingers. Then the gas would not light, and she would fumble wastefully with matches, and almost certainly the baby would cry and then he would drum the fingers of his good hand, and there would not be a clean nappy, or Ivy and Lily, infected by her frantic

2

apron-wiping and her wide frightened eyes, would begin to whimper, or worse, to quarrel, and she would be almost frozen by all the things to do and his relentless stare and the rapid drubbing of his fingers on the table. And it would build and build until her mother came in, and then it would look like chaos and there would be the mother's quick, reproachful look, then the tired thin face hardening, resigned, turning to him and then it would start.

Perhaps crockery would not be smashed, yet. Perhaps it would be the verbal lashing, the children silent, huddled, making themselves as small as possible behind the big armchair. 'Slut!' he would call their mother, and Grace. 'Slovenly whores, fit for the gutters!' His abuse, in his tight cockney voice, had an oratorical rhythm, rising and falling, building in volume, the practised curses rolling out, the end inevitable – the snatched overcoat, the slammed door, the room shivering, silent behind him. The mother, tight-lipped, would put on her apron, finish the stew; Grace would finally and competently get on with her chores. Then, it would be a race against time, the odds depending on how much money was in his pocket.

They would eat, carefully, slowly, not looking at the clock. If he could only stay out until after the baby's feed, then everyone could be in bed pretending sleep when he came in. Not that this always worked – he had been known to rage through the children's room, too, flailing indiscriminately, Grace trying to block the blows as she vaguely remembered her mother doing for her when she was small. She would not let herself think about what happened in the other small bedroom on the nights when she lay with the pillow pressed around her ears desperately not hearing the thuds, the

3

muffled crashes, her mother's unwilling, half-stifled cries. She had been used, all her life, to the fading and fresh bruises on her mother's thin body as she washed in her slip in the mornings.

That is the way the girls grew up. When the 1914–18 war ended Grace was almost twelve. She was still at the Dame school, helping with the younger pupils, Ivy and Lily and Maude among them. The baby, Olive, was still at home. Grace had been offered a scholarship to high school, but her father said they couldn't afford it. He was impatient for her twelfth birthday, when she could be put to earning money.

The war had not made much difference to the way they lived. Other people's fathers, brothers, uncles, husbands fought, died sometimes, but Grace's father, Clive, was exempt because of his arm. He had a better job, entrenched in the military-support system, and the mother, big Olive (little, thin Olive), cleaned and made beds in the hospital. She had stopped having babies. Things were easier – or they would have been without Clive. Little Olive was a delight, charming and spoilt in the family's new comfort. Growing up to call herself Olivia, the only one to finish high school, she would never be beaten with a wooden arm, would remember her father with fondness.

Grace did not want to leave the school. She had discovered a love of reading there, a cleverness that could not be destroyed by Clive's frustrated anger. She had a friend too, a young teacher, to whom she had recently learned to pour out her fear and bewilderment. But how her friend had paled, grown smaller, faced with Clive in the crowded living-room.

'How much?' he said, cunning, red-faced.

4

'Well, not much at first,' said Miss Green, hesitantly. She was very young, poor herself. 'But she'd be getting her training, and her meal in the middle of the day.'

'How much is not much?' And when he was told he laughed angrily. 'She's been working there for nothing as it is, for two years.'

'But, that's because you wouldn't . . . because she couldn't go to high school. And she couldn't work for wages until now.'

'No. Bloody soft the lot of you. I was out working, in all weather, long before I was ten, with a few pence and a cuff over the earlobes *if* I was lucky.'

'But in a few years . . . if she passed her exams, she'd be earning pounds.'

'Well I can't afford a few years. I've sweated my guts out keeping her this long as it is. And bloody little to show for it, too. Keeps house like a trollop, her nose in a book all day – her poor mother working her fingers to the bone. No. She goes to the milliner, *and* thinks herself lucky.'

One more day, tearful, to give back the borrowed books, say her goodbyes, avoiding Letty Green's guilty sympathy, the grimy sad faces of her 'bubbas' class. But she had her dress, a pale blue pinafore, made for her, not altered from one of her mother's, and a woollen jacket as well. The old man had been grim, realising the money kept from him by Olive in her determination to see Grace decently turned out for her job. He had given in, however, even to the shoes, although he insisted on two sizes too large so they wouldn't go to waste. And Grace, even then, in her ill-cut hardly fitting clothes, was beautiful, with her pale oval face, her large slanting eyes and her cloud of deep red hair.

By the time she was fourteen, now apprenticed to

a seamstress, she could contrive cheap elegance from remnants and, by taking an extra half-hour and saving her bus fare, could afford cotton stockings. Ivy was out of school by then too, working as a shop-girl in a haberdashery, and the two would walk down the narrow road together through London's busy mornings, quite pleased with themselves and the little rosettes and bows they tied on after leaving the house.

They had their admirers already, Grace with her creamy slim charm and Ivy, black-eyed and Roman-nosed, already the wit with her cockney quickness and merry laugh. Girls grew up quickly in those crowded back streets, but neither of them would have ever dared let the old man know about the sharp-faced youths who walked them to the corner in the afternoons or loitered at lamp-posts for the chance of a brief and saucy exchange.

As they got older they got braver, and sometimes stayed out to see one of the tuppenny shows or eat greasy hot fish and chips in the frosty park. The old man did not always catch them, but if he did, out would come the arm and his scathing abuse. One evening their bus didn't come and they ran home from the Odeon, breathless with fear and appalled laughter. He didn't believe their story, and when the next day's newspaper told of the bus strike he simply said: 'Well, that'll do you for the times I don't know about.'

Their fear of him gradually turned to contempt, and they began to talk back, intervening for their mother. His fine bully's rages turned sour in the face of their young strength and he took to glowering through their chatter, finally driven to spend more time alone at the pub, puzzled at the loss of his power, wondering how a look from Ivy's bright eyes or Grace's hand stilled suddenly at her cooking could somehow lower his upraised fist towards Olive. 'Pack of bitches,' he would complain to his cronies, 'a man's home's not his own any more.'

There was laughter in the flat now as the girls drew Olive into their small conspiracies, repeated the gossip of the streets, tried out new hairdos and did things to their eyebrows with tweezers and black pencil. But the cheerful faces would become blank when he walked in and his own clumsy attempts at jollity, his pathetic wish to be part of it, would be met with bland gazes and perhaps a quick whisper and a giggle. He tried appealing to the younger girls, but Maude and Lily were too lost in admiration of their big sisters to pay him any attention. Little Olive was the only one too young to understand the careful, hostile wrenching away of his dominance, and she became his pet. He brought her toys and fancies done up in tissue paper, not realising that anything, anything that eroded his arrogance was fuel to the others' fire, nor that their own love for the baby made them glad for her sake.

Grace changed her job without telling him and went off to the Lyons Corner House now at all hours in a smart short black dress and silk stockings. Ivy kept back enough of her wages to go to an evening class in typing and shorthand and his grumbles were ignored. Lily took a two-year scholarship to the high school – Olive signed the permission and Clive again was not consulted. He could hardly bear it, the evenings of Grace bent over the table cutting out the pinafores and blouses for Lily's uniform, the giggling and preening as she tried them on, and Olive, always passive, now with a triumphant gleam about everything she did.

His threats turned to bluster, even on the nights, more and more frequent, when he rolled home drunk and found the bedroom door locked against him and a quilt thrown carelessly on the couch. He was tolerated: they cooked his meals and ironed his collars and darned his socks as they always had, but they paid him no attention. Olive had begun to look smarter too, with Grace making little crocheted collars for her sombre dresses, Ivy bringing her home a plaited silk belt, both girls persuading her to use a little lipstick and colour on her cheeks. He began to look at Olive again, but she had been waiting a long time for her revenge. When he suggested that they both get spruced up and go down the pub for a pie, she refused, saying she would rather go to the pictures with the girls. Somehow it became accepted that now he always slept on the couch.

Grace was earning good money, and plenty of tips, and she had her hair done every week at a salon. She was walking out with a young man who worked at the butcher's, but Clive had not met him. When he complained to Olive she was calm, and said he seemed a decent enough chap.

'I suppose I'll get an invite to the wedding,' he said to Grace, but she ignored the sarcasm.

'I expect you'll have to,' she said, and her pertness silenced him.

But before any weddings, there was the row. The girls had set themselves to spying on him, trying to find out where he spent the couple of nights a week when he did not come home at all, and some evenings Ivy and Grace would be collapsed with laughter as they followed his stumbling cursing figure up the hill to their block of flats, holding each other helplessly as they watched him fumbling for his key, made out his muttered self-pity and threats under the glow of the gas lamp.

'No one cares for the poor old bugger,' they would overhear, stuffing their handkerchiefs into their mouths, 'No one cares. Work all your bloody life for nothing . . . they'll be sorry. Bloody man's entitled to a bit of comfort, in't he? Hey, in't he?' and he would bend shakily to the battered tom-cat on the steps, call him his mate, sympathise with him also at the mercies of bloody-minded females.

But it was Lily who found out. And Grace walked into the uneasy shocked silence of the living-room guessing immediately that this was something that might not be laughed away.

'We've found out what he's doing,' Ivy said, her bitter mouth very like Olive's as she lit one of the cigarettes she had recently begun to smoke.

'Well? What?' Grace assumed it was some woman somewhere, they more or less hoped it was, it might get him off their hands for good.

'Lily saw him coming out on her way to school this morning.'

'Yes, he saw me too, and all.' Lily was excited, but Grace couldn't understand the mystery.

'Well? Who is it then? Old Peg?' They all smiled at that. 'They'd bloody suit each other, she could hit him with her wig.'

'It's Letty Green,' said Olive. 'Poor little devil.'

'Bloody hell!' said Grace, and they relaxed when they saw she was not upset.

But when Clive came in later, sheepish and defiant, it was Grace who gave him his marching orders. They had packed up all his clothes into paper bags and stacked them by the door, and when he started shouting, Grace stood with her hand on the doorknob and said she would get the janitor and have him thrown down the stairs. Olive said nothing, watched him with an expression of grim satisfaction, but Grace heard her weeping later in the night.

The three older girls took it in turn from then on to wait at the warehouse gates on pay-nights, watching carefully as the old man counted out Olive's housekeeping, ignoring his ingratiating enquiries, although Ivy sometimes would tell him tartly that they were all a damn sight better off without him. Grace occasionally found herself wondering, though, about Olive, who seemed to have become smaller and more wrinkled suddenly. Little Olive missed him, and gradually Ivy and Grace accepted that he might sometimes be in the flat when they got in of an evening, clearly having eaten there, and gradually his presence at Sunday dinner became a habit, too, where he behaved politely, an uneasy visitor, bringing Olive flowers and sometimes a bottle of stout. He never suggested moving back, despite his wistful stares, and they never mentioned Letty Green's name.

Letty came into the restaurant one night when Grace was working but Grace said she was too busy to talk, and swept past, to and fro, with piled trays, swishing her flared skirt, flirting and laughing with her regulars, until Letty with a pale resigned face sat at a little table by the window and ordered tea and toast.

Grace came with the food and stood impatiently with Letty's hand on her arm.

10

'I'd like to try and . . . explain.'

'There's no need,' Grace tapped her red fingernails on her order pad.

'Gracie . . . I was so lonely here, so miserable. You can't know what it's been like.'

'No? Well, I wish you luck of *him*. He's a right one to make anybody happy.' And she was off down the aisle to the beer salesman who always left a heavy tip, keeping it up, the graceful swagger and her demurely pert repartee until out of the corner of her eye she saw Letty pay at the desk and slink out, hunch-shouldered. Then Grace allowed herself to slump against the wall in the kitchen and tremble a little until someone asked if she was all right and she laughed, 'Yes. Just something nasty crawled out of the woodpile.'

She didn't mention the visit at home, but heard how Letty had come to see Olive, too, and how Olive with quiet pride had made her a cup of tea and calmed her down, and offered to do the old man's laundry.

'You what?' Grace laughing in anger.

'Well, I'm used to it. I don't mind. And you know how fussy he is about his collars. That poor gormless thing couldn't even hold the iron.'

'And *he* comes out of it all right, too, doesn't he? Playtime with his little floozie and you still looking after him!'

Grace argued, but was baffled by Olive's obstinacy, admitting finally to Ivy that she didn't bloody understand what was going on.

'If it makes our mum happy it's all right, isn't it?'

'Happy!' But she let it drop. She had her own worries. The butcher's apprentice wanted to get married, but she had been seeing someone else and there was bound to be a collision any time now. Ivy pursed her lips and told her she would have to make some sort of decision soon, but Grace laughed and said they'd probably make it for her – it was getting so that she couldn't remember who she'd arranged to meet, or where, in the evenings. She was enjoying it, Ivy thought, and why shouldn't she? Pretty, laughing Gracie, it was about time she had some fun. Ivy herself had already begun what was to be a lifelong affair with a man married to an invalid Catholic wife and was teaching herself stoicism in rapid, painful stages. She was waiting for Grace to decide who she was going to marry – it seemed easier somehow for Ivy to move into her own rooms if one of them was married and respectable.

And in the end it was Ted, not the butcher's lad, that Grace chose. He was older, the foreman in a factory, and he had some savings. He wanted Grace to stop work when they married and said he'd got enough for a little house in the suburbs. Ivy was sceptical at the image of Grace settling to that, but she said nothing. Ted clearly, as she said, thought the sun shone out of Grace's backside.

At the wedding, with Grace in pale satin and her hair newly bobbed, Ivy thought she certainly seemed happy enough. The old man had paid handsomely for the whole thing and stood around jovial in his pin-stripes and bow-tie, urging champagne on everyone. It was hard to believe the frightful tyrant he had been, but the older girls kept the memories fresh in their bitter stories. Only little Olive, now at high school, they protected, letting her enjoy his indulgences and rambling sentimentality.

Ivy waited until Grace and Ted were back from their seaside honeymoon – 'Bloody damp sheets and gnat

bites everywhere,' Grace said, but she was glowing –
and then told Olive she was going to get a bedsitter
which she would probably share with a girlfriend. She
would go on paying Olive a small amount each week
and she and Grace promised each other to keep an eye
on things so that the old bugger didn't sneak back in
behind their backs.

Grace and Ted moved to their redbrick cottage and
Grace busied herself with curtains and chair-covers and
discovered a natural talent for gardening. She was pregnant within weeks of the marriage, Ted was bursting with
pride and love, and Ivy, crossing her fingers, thought
that perhaps it was all just what Grace had needed.

2
————————

My mother's name was Grace; she was graceful. I have
a photograph of her that used to stand on the piano
with one of my father thin-lipped in his naval uniform.
Hers is of a woman in her flowering: high cheek-bones,
wide hopeful blue eyes, soft red marcelled hair. There
is a glow about her in this picture, but that may be
the hand-tinting.

She used to potter about her garden in a floral print overall, a buttoning dress with short sleeves like a dressing-gown, but respectable to wear during the day. She weeded and planted, and muttered to her fowls pecking in the loose earth that marked her progress.

They were her happiest times, in her garden, the cat on a fence-post somewhere near, the dog lying in a patch of shade. She had green thumbs, everyone said so. The stakes she cut to hold the dahlias often sprouted and became small trees. The cuttings she plucked from any garden she passed grew and flowered profusely. Her thyme never seeded, but became a perennial bush; honeysuckle climbed sweetly over the tankstand, the pinks and lobelia in her borders did not need re-bedding, never developed the sparse brown patches that had to be planted again. Nectarines loaded the old tree every summer; gooseberries formed an impenetrable hedge down by the old dunny, hydrangea burgeoned sky-blue all through the garden. There were six rose bushes, won in a raffle, that bloomed crimson, pale yellow, fragrant and rich, for most of the year.

Grace had a purple taffeta dress that she wore on Christmas Eve or someone's birthday. Perhaps when I was very young she wore it to dances or parties with my father. Sometimes she let me try it on; it swirled stiff radiant colours around me.

Grace wore rouge in pink round spots and bright scarlet lipstick. She chain-smoked menthol cigarettes and swore; she was a cockney. She drank Guinness and hid the bottles in the kitchen cupboards from my father. She laughed with her mouth wide open – sometimes you could see the dentures. Even in old age, after two strokes, she was pretty.

14

When I was little she was warm and held me often; later she became complaining, complicit and hesitant. She said she would not leave my father because she wouldn't give him the satisfaction. On Saturday and Sunday mornings I woke usually to the sound of their bitter raised voices. Other mornings he went to work early and Grace and I had breakfast quietly together. On weekends he followed her about the house nagging, until her muttered replies against his deafness irritated him into shouting. They had separate bedrooms.

Grace told stories. Of London during the war, before the war. Of her father, who had a wooden arm; of growing up in a slum, with a leaking toilet on every second floor. How the father beat the girls, when he was drunk, with his spare arm. She laughed, telling about it, but it wasn't funny at the time. (The fingers hurt most, cruel and stiff, though the back of the wooden hand could still bruise.) And there was the bloke on the floor below who thought he was Napoleon and would make his wife and children strip naked and salute in a straight line.

She never spoke of her first marriage, her other children. I found out about them accidentally, when I was fifteen. Instead she smiled, slyly, remembering the munitions factory and the chocolates and stockings addressed to her that came down the conveyor belt.

Grace could play the piano by ear and by 'vamping' and still sang the old songs – 'A Long Way to Tipperary', 'K-K-K-Katie', 'Lili Marlene' – that came from the time of the photograph, her flowering, but I didn't know her then . . .

Grace, in apricot silk, dusting the piano, sang. The room shone; dim lights and the blackout curtains made its shabbiness mysterious – still, empty, waiting, like Grace herself, inside. Ourwardly she flickered, in and out of the lamp's circle, the creamy light washing over the shining folds of her dress, her pale arms, the deep waving red hair.

She looked into the scalloped mirror above the fire-place. Crimson nails patted combs into place, her lipsticked mouth pursed, a perfect cupid's bow. She smoothed the dress over her hips, felt a roughness on her hand catch the material, frowned. At thirty-five she was slim; padded shoulders suited her, made her gaunt-ness elegant, but she wished the short skirts of her youth were still fashionable, to show off her legs in the silk stockings the Australian had brought from America.

She heard the tap in the other room, her friend mak-ing tea. She looked once round the room again and, satisfied, went to join Coral in the kitchen.

He leaned on the mantelpiece in his naval uniform, watching. He was older than the others in the room and he wouldn't dance because Grace was still at the piano in a circle of light and gaiety. Young men in khaki stood around her, singing and laughing, jostling to turn the pages of her music. Her sister, Ivy, just off-duty and still in uniform, sat half on the piano-stool, her eyes closed, mouthing the words of the song, her shoulder against the thigh of one of the young soldiers. Two or three cou-ples danced slowly in and out of the shadows, occasion-ally bumping the rolled carpet under the windows.

Ivy opened her eyes and saw him watching. She smiled and got up.

'I'll give Gracie a spell in a minute,' she said. 'Then

you can have her to yourself.'

He gave his thin-lipped grin that turned his rather serious face cheeky. Ivy reminded him of his younger sister, Alice, at home in Adelaide knitting lumpy brown socks for her brothers and young husband away at the war.

'Don't you lot ever sleep?' he said. 'No one would think there was a war on.'

'Got to keep our spirits up. And theirs,' she waved, laughing, towards the uniformed youths. 'Talking of which, I'll get you another brandy.'

When Ivy took her turn at the piano, he and Grace sat on the sofa together, Grace turning her shoulders to the young men who wanted to dance. He leaned away from her slightly, watching the lovely line of cheek and jaw, the shadow of her hair on her pale back.

She gulped her drink down and put her hand on his knee. She wanted to dance. He knew she was putting off the time when they would have to talk, but they only had tonight – he was due back at his ship the next day and her husband's leave started soon. It was her decision, he had already made his. He felt cold fear that he would not have her, after all, but he let her pull him to his feet, and holding her gently, very close, he danced with her.

The room was empty again, waiting, his silence a pressure on her as she dawdled about picking up dirty glasses, clearing ashtrays, avoiding Bill waiting on the sofa. Coral came in, looked at them, said good-night hastily. Grace walked to the window, almost lifted the curtain to look out, then remembering, stood with her arms folded staring at the black velvet inches from her eyes.

17

'Grace?'

She turned her back further on him. It was all happening too quickly. She didn't really want to have to decide, not yet, not to have to think, attempt to shape the future. She wanted to drink some more, play the piano, then go to bed with this thin, earnest man. But she knew if she was not prepared to decide now she would not see him again, and she was not ready for that. He loved her in a way new to her, not jocosely, taking her for granted, like the other men she had known, like her husband, but with awe, with gratitude, with a sort of hysterical delight. He would give up everything: his family, his settled middle-class security, his country even, for this one chance with her.

She could feel his whole serious will concentrated on her now, waiting for her to speak. She knew that what she said could transport him, or break him utterly. She stroked her bare arms, and like a cat responded instantly to her own touch. She wanted him, she would have him.

'I'll tell Ted,' she said, muttering into the curtains. 'I'll tell him. First thing.'

Then she turned, swooped quickly to him, kissed his mouth to stop the flow of words.

'We'll work it out later. Be quiet now, it's late, I'm tired. Let's go to bed.' Her quick Londoner's voice was blurred with fatigue, perhaps a faint discontent, but he didn't notice in his relief. Now he could let himself think about the woman, the sons, the airy sandstone house in the wide Adelaide street that he had already given up. Now he knew what it was to be replaced by. It would not now be the tight empty place in his mind that he would not dare to approach. In the morning he could go back to his ship, happy, resolved. He could write his wife another letter, this time with pity and some affection. He could let himself weep a little for the boys who would grow up without him. Now he had Grace.

He began undressing her before they reached the bedroom. He could be active now, dominant. And Grace, bending to him with her large smile, her gentle sensuality, pushed aside her anxiety as she gave in to the pleasure, the passion. She refused to think, crossing her fingers that it would all be all right, it would work out somehow. Turning out the light she gave herself up to the caresses, the adoration, the wonder in his voice as repeated his love.

Bill was the second oldest of five sons and daughters of northern English migrants who had settled the Adelaide Hills in the 1890s. The oldest boy, Morris, and Bill were still babies when the family arrived, the others were born in Australia.

This is the way they grew up: first the father bought some land, acres beyond the dreams of an Englishman, with assistance from the government. Labour was cheap then, there were many itinerants who would work for months for hardly more than their board and lodging, who would loaf off to other work in season, and come back year after year for the lambing or the fruit-picking. The father, old Bill, was shrewd. His family had been Scottish crofters who had lost their land through endless bad seasons and had settled in the dense factory areas over the border where they could find work. But old Bill had never lost the feel for the land that had informed his childhood; he had always known he would farm again, some day. His wife, Ethel, came from better stock, a laird's clan, but her family was also part of the impoverished migration south, and she had always been used to back-breaking work and long hours. They were wiry Scottish protestants, and twice migrants they had the migrant's fierce resolve to build a better life for themselves and a bright future for their children.

Bill and his brothers and sisters grew up on horseback, or in the floorspaces of horse-drawn ploughs. Carried in a sling at their mother's breast, or piggybacked by their father as he strode around the fences, they grew up knowing every inch of their land, every animal and every tree. The work of the farm began as play, being allowed to 'help', and merged without notice into the real chores of the place. The girls could feed the fowls as soon as they could toddle; Bill remembered all his life the time, when at the age of eight, his father made him bury the dead lamb whose mother's teats it had been his responsibility to check.

The work on the farm was hard, but it was as natural as breathing to them, and if there was not much laughter there was peace, good food, abundant fruit and vegetables from their own soil, a daily sense of accomplishment and growth.

Every Sunday old Bill would harness the dray and they would ride the two-hour journey into Adelaide to the Presbyterian church. By the time young Bill was about ten the family was beginning to prosper, and on Sundays Ethel wore a draped long woollen skirt with a handsome jacket and her mother's pearl brooch on the lapel; the boys had their suits and soft cotton shirts and the girls wore smocks of fine printed linen. They were brought up god-fearing, in that practical Scottish way, to unquestioning obedience towards old Bill and calm respect for their mother, Ethel; to the auto-matic assumption that clean hard-working lives would lead to plenty on earth and a reward in heaven.

The house became Ethel's domain, now that they could afford hired labour, and it had grown over the years from a simple two-roomed cabin to a gracious farmhouse with wide verandahs and polished, cool rooms. The boys still helped work the place before and after school and on weekends, and the girls did the housework and learned to cook and tended the domes-tic animals and the gardens. Ethel bought a piano, and in the evenings, after their generous dinner in the scrubbed kitchen, the family would sit in the parlour while she played the folk ballads of her youth and they all sang. Young Bill was given a flute and in time he would accompany his mother, the poignant, sentimen-tal threads of 'Annie Laurie' or 'Bonny Doon', floating out into the warm shadows of the garden.

They all worked hard at school – they had been taught to work hard at everything – and they did well. When war broke out in 1914, Morris was already at the university with a brilliant future predicted for him. There was no question as to whether he would join up, and he enlisted for the Light Horse on the first day they called for volunteers.

He had one 48-hour leave before he went, and old Bill went with him back to Adelaide to watch the loading of the horses on to the ship, and see him off. Young Bill brooded around the farm for a few days, then asked his mother for his birth certificate. By the weekend he was gone and when old Bill returned he and Ethel had the first row the children could remember in their presence.

'He's too young.' Ethel could barely control her fear for her first-born, now she was helpless at the thought of her dreamy-eyed sixteen-year-old lost to her.

'He's a man,' old Bill said; he was bursting with pride for his sons, had got a photographer in Adelaide to make a portrait of Morris in his uniform with his gleaming riding boots and the crop held against his leg in one gloved hand. 'But,' glaring at ten-year-old Alec, 'don't you think you're going to do anything daft, either.'

'You *bloody* men,' it was the first time, too, they had ever heard her swear. 'With your wars and your politics.' She was a fierce liberal herself, she and Bill had both joined the Labor Party, but nothing, not the Hun, nor later the Turk, and their threat to European freedom, was worth the thought of her sons in danger.

Bill came back four weeks later for the weekend, trudging up the dusty road in his spotless khaki, gaiters, slouch hat rakishly over one eyebrow. He had altered his birth certificate, and, being tall for his age, no one had asked questions. He was enjoying the army, had become a kind of pet in the barracks with his cheerful innocence and his willingness to play the flute for sing-songs. They were shipping off soon, but he couldn't tell the family where they were going.

He sat about edgily in the parlour with his admiring sisters, or walked around the property with the old man who to Bill's embarrassment, passed on worldly advice about brothels and army life. Blushing, kicking at tussocks with his polished army boots, Bill wished himself back at camp, where he was in with a decent, manly group of youths, who read their bibles in the evening or pored over simple letters from childhood sweethearts, and talked of the war with shining-eyed idealism.

Ethel kept herself aloof this weekend, afraid if she

relaxed it would all come pouring out, her terrible fears, but when the boy left she gave him a leather-bound copy of Housman and the three pairs of thick socks she had managed to knit in the last few weeks.

Bill's division formed part of the Second Landing at Gallipoli, and he struggled up the beach as friends were mown down from the sandhills. *The Shropshire Lad* gave him comfort in the months that followed, in the filthy trenches, the ingenuous Christian aphorisms reminding him of home among the bloody confusion of almost daily battles.

Finally, with shrapnel wounds that might have cost him his legs, he was invalided out to a hospital in Marseilles, where he spend the rest of the war, stunned, gratefully flirting with the French nurses who comforted him in his nightmares.

He came home to Australian summer at the end of the war, walking with sticks, gaunt, much older than twenty. Morris had been killed in the first six months; Bill was now the oldest son. It took him many weeks, limping, soaking up the warmth and sunshine, his mother's lavish cooking, before he could begin to think of what he might do now. Mary, his next sister, was already training to be a nurse, with some irritation that the war had ended before she could join it. Alec and Alice were at high school; the farm was prospering, a township was growing up nearby, everything seemed to have grown, bigger, cleaner, while he has been away.

He could go to the university, Ethel suggested, there were government scholarships for returned soldiers, but he would have to prepare for matriculation at night-school. He agreed, listlessly, but meanwhile got a part-time job in a motor garage where he discovered a love and a talent for machinery. He decided he would go to the technical college and study mechanical engineering. There he made graphs and neat plans lettered in his careful Edwardian script, his large sensitive hands already bruised and scratched from the practical side of the course, taking motors apart, putting them together again, tinkering with farm machinery when he was home.

He swam in the river and the dams whenever he could and rode the one horse they had kept now that they had a motor tractor and a stern, upright car, and gradually the muscle came back to his legs, though they stiffened painfully if he lay for too long under the car chassis fiddling with its workings.

When his course was finished he said he had a mind to see some of the country, and for the next five years he was on the move, gold-mining, digging for opals at Coober Pedy, settling for a while at a granary as a mechanic, and for one peaceful year working as the engineer on the Murray paddle steamers. Through all this he came back regularly to the farm, saw Mary married, advised nineteen-year-old Alec who was at the tech doing the same engineering course and had never lost his childish desire to be a train-driver, took a photograph of Alice when she first wore her probationer's cap, and, occasionally now, played his flute with his mother again in the evenings.

He had just signed on for another six months on the steamers when he met Carrie at a church bazaar. His mother watched the courting with satisfaction. Carrie, long-limbed, athletic, from a similar background to their own, had just finished her teacher training and had come to work in the little school in the township. Bill went off for his weekly trips down the river, and Carrie visited with Ethel and Alice at the farm while he was away. The old man began to hint that he could come up with a small bit of capital if Bill wanted to settle down to something.

It was a large and very suitable wedding. The Kerrs were almost what passed for society in the Hills now, Ethel on many women's committees, old Bill an office-holder in the local Labor Party branch. Carrie's family, business people, had also relatives who were on the land and she had spent much of her childhood on their farm. She said, tentatively, to Bill that she wouldn't mind a small place with some sheep and goats and perhaps a market garden, but he was already negotiating for the lease on the first motor garage in the township. This he paid for with his own savings; he had led a simple and ascetic life during his wanderings, but old Bill gave them the large block of land in the new suburb being built down the hills towards Adelaide and said he would pay for the building of a house.

Meanwhile they lived with his family and Carrie continued to teach. After trips to the quarries and long involved talks with Mary's husband, an architect, studying the blueprints late into the night, Bill thought he could build most of the house himself. The family joined in with enthusiasm, and weekends became gay hard-working picnics, the women trundling the heavy sandstone in wheelbarrows, the men stripped to the waist, or in overalls, shouting cheerfully to each other, subduing their curses if the women were near. The house began to rise around them, the large rooms with their long window-holes began to be called the parlour, or the main bedroom, or the sunroom. They ate their bread and cheese and purple grapes at dusk in the still roofless dining-room, off a board over rough trestles. Carrie and Bill often stayed after the others had left, walking hand in hand through the half-finished house, deciding what furniture they would need and where. In the last weeks, before they gave over the work to the plasterers and carpenters, they decided on the second small bedroom for the baby. They were hoping the house would be finished for their first child.

In the next years Bill bought two more garages and installed managers; his sons appeared regularly every two years, and the beautiful house, now filled with lovely furniture, much of it a present from Carrie's parents, was also full of the laughter and noise of little boys. Bill stopped having his frightful nightmares, he enjoyed the evenings when Carrie entertained the local doctor and his wife or the minister, their prim, neat maid waiting on table, the good silver and crockery shining under the modest chandelier, then the gramophone playing Bach, Mozart, and Bill's favourite, Ravel's *Bolero*. Sometimes they would have their coffee on the terrace and gaze over the smooth lawn at the young trees and Carrie's roses, the air thick with the smell of gardenia or jasmine, the wrought iron around the verandahs already tangled in heavy wisteria and purple and green bearing grapevines.

The Kerrs were still a close family, and on Sundays they took it in turns to serve the heavy midday dinners, going to Mary's or to Bill and Ethel, or to Alec and his new wife Beatie further out past the hills where they lived with Beatie's old father and helped run the vineyard while Alec studied for his train-driver's certificate. The years of the depression were kind to them, they had no mortgages and they were not subject to what old Bill called wage slavery. The family did what they could, donating generously to local funds for the unemployed, always finding an odd job or a few weeks work for the thin, hopeless men and sometimes women who came anxiously to the gate with their belongings tied on their backs. Carrie kept bundles of her own and Bill's old clothing washed and mended, for such people and taught the boys always to put a few pennies in the poor box at the church and to give away some of their last year's toys at Christmas. If Bill sometimes felt, restlessly, talking to the grim, wandering men who occupied the bungalow for a few weeks, doing the gardening and visibly putting on condition with Carrie's cooking, that he might like to hump his bluey too and take to the track with only his own wits and strength and his copy of Housman, he knew, with a certain complacence, that it was not possible. He had a chain of garages now, and four growing boys who needed him, not to mention his old parents, who were growing frail.

3
_____

My father's name was John William Kerr, but he had always been called Bill. His photograph is not the one that stood with my mother's on the piano, it is the yellowed print taken before he went to Gallipoli. In it he looks like Leslie Howard, sensitive, long-nosed, gaitered, the digger's hat slung casually over one shoulder. That was his time, probably, his flowering, except that the youth who went to that war were not allowed to bloom: dirt and degradation and horror nipped them in the bud. Decent boys from clean houses up to their knees in blood, pus, urine and rats.

I never really knew Bill; he was elderly already when I was born, never played cricket with us or chasing games like other fathers, only sometimes around and around the house after me to give me a belting for some misdemeanour.

He grew up in the Adelaide Hills and must have had an ordinary, pleasant childhood, working the farm, going to school, catching tadpoles in the dams. I still don't know how old he was when he died – his birth certificate had been changed at least twice, the first time to go to the first war at sixteen to join his older brother, the second to get into the British Merchant Marine in 1939, since even with backward forgery he was too old for the Australian services.

He would tell his 'yarns' sometimes, if there were people visiting, or if I asked him about something in his photograph albums full of little black and white snaps with their white-ink captions in his careful writing and little flourishes. The yarns were about his childhood, or his travels; people he had known on the ships, never the business of those merchantmen travelling heavy submarine-haunted seas in wartime.

He gave me the collected works of Robert Burns for my twelfth birthday: it was a legend in his family that his mother had owned original Burns manuscripts but that later, when his father was senile and alone at the homestead, taking in derelicts and vagabonds, they must have been stolen. I visited that grandfather once, in his old man's home – he had ginger drooping moustaches, he dribbled bewilderment. He thought I was one of his daughters made a child again.

Bill was wounded at Gallipoli and spent the rest of the war in a French hospital, where they saved his legs. His nightmares when I knew him were all of the Turks, the bloody Turks coming over the next sand-dune. Even after being sunk three times in that other war, almost trapped in engine rooms. His legs ached, often, when he was old. I remember them, white, scrawny, still shrapnel-scarred, when we took our infrequent trips to the beach. His skinny legs, his old man's stoop, his navy-blue woollen bathers.

'Thought the bloody sun shone out of you when you were a kiddie, he did,' Grace would say to me sometimes, in a grumbling tone, as if somehow this were another piece of ammunition in the slack weapon of her hatred for him. But I don't remember that, only flashes of riding on the trailer when he went to collect

29

wood, watching him boil the billy, sometimes going with him when he checked the machinery at the cool store, being allowed to ride on the heavy apple trolleys. Sitting with him sometimes on the couch while we looked at the photos and he told me about exotic places, women in kimonos, Indians, opal miners.

He'd been peripatetic, adventuring, in the years between the wars: the photos of the young gold-miner, the timber cutter, the Murray steamer sailor no longer show the dreamy idealistic eyes of the child who went to Gallipoli. They are squinted up by then, as I remember them, against hope, perhaps. Somewhere he'd married, fathered sons, bought garages, prospered. Like Grace, he kept no pictures of that life. The second war must have been a last grasp at what he sensed was out there, had been held from him.

No, my memories of Bill are soured, obscured by Grace's muttering vindictive presence. I loved her so much, my vulgar laughing mother, sided with her against his brooding disappointment. He was the villain of our lives, the no-sayer to our pleasure. I only began to realise what he might be, might have been, shortly before he died, still dream him alive in sweaty nights of guilt. But by the time he died I had inevitably turned out wrong, as everything had, not what he'd meant at all . . .

It was to Ivy's little bedsitting-room with its smell of cheap fish that Grace went when everything started to go wrong.

You've always been the sensible one,' Grace was

wry, but her eyes were frightened. 'So what the bloody hell do I do now?'

Ivy's uniform hung from the screen that hid the bed, and she sat in her Chinese-blue dressing-gown at the small table beside Grace. Grace still pushed at her eyes with a damp handkerchief, but she had stopped the ugly sobbing of her first attempts to speak.

Ivy lit a cigarette and passed it to her sister, saw the smudge of unblotted crimson round its tip when Grace put it down. She'd always wished Grace would be tidier in her habits. She looked at the window. It was raining, sleeting, London grey and wet and ruined. Ivy shivered, the heating in the flat was unreliable. She wished she were not the one others always came to for advice. Her own life was messy enough, God knew, her man who would never marry her, who would go back to his wife in the country when the war was over.

'Oh Gracie. Didn't you realise Ted would fight to keep the kiddies? Did you even think about it?' She looked at her sister and sighed. She thought with a sudden pang how *she* would miss the boys – she knew she would never have her own. She almost said, accusingly, that Grace could have other children.

Grace sniffed, and the tears began to run again. Of course she had thought about it, vaguely; had seen herself and Bill, somewhere, a sunny place, and the boys running about on a green lawn.

'Come on, buck up old dear.' Ivy put her arm around Grace's shoulders and hugged her close. 'I expect it's too late to change your mind? About Bill, I mean?' But of course it was, she thought. Dreamy, compliant, laughing Grace – she could be as obstinate as a pig when she had set her mind on something as she had apparently set her mind on this Australian sailor. And Ted, Ivy knew, would be unforgiving, with the law to back him up.

They sat, rocking, comforting each other until Grace stopped crying and their bitter, familial humour struggled to the surface.

'Well, I suppose I've only got myself to blame,' Grace said, attempting a laugh. A favourite remark of their mother's.

'Yes, and there's no good crying over split milk.'

'You've got to laugh, haven't you?' (Because, if you don't laugh, you'll cry.)

She described Ted's face when she'd told him, how he'd dropped his beer on the kitchen floor and stood, his braces down around his thighs, his mouth open in astonishment in the growing puddle at his stockinged feet.

'Well,' seeing Ivy's sad look, 'I've made my bed, now I must lie in it.' Her wide mouth twisting almost to its usual generous shape, Ivy's arm tightening on her shoulder, both nearly hysterical now, laughing, Ivy's long fingers gripping Grace's arm, holding it down, holding *her* down.

Bill got compassionate leave, to be with Grace until her divorce. She was already pregnant, and she had moved to a little flat with Bill in the same building as Ivy's rooms. Ted would not let her see the boys, the two sons of her four married pregnancies. Her first child had miscarried, the second had died of pneumonia while a baby. She wrote to the boys nearly every day, telling them she hoped they'd be with her soon, to make sure they wrapped up well in the cold winter, but she had no way of knowing if they ever got her letters.

She and Bill took the train once, to the country town where the children had been evacuated to, but the woman at the farmhouse was unhelpful. There was a court order, she said, staring at Grace's bulky stomach. She didn't really see how she could do anything. Grace was sure that one of the voices in the noisy barn was Tommy's, but Bill stopped her from pushing past the forbidding woman to see.

'If there's a court order,' he said, 'it might go against you at the divorce.'

So she stumbled, blinded with tears, back to the station and the train to London.

After the divorce, Grace crying noisily through the whole thing – 'adultery', 'custody to the father', visiting rights to be arranged – Bill went back to the war, to be sunk again and stranded in Canada. Grace lived alone, pregnant and ill, in the flat he paid the rent for, waiting.

One night, caught shopping a mile from the flat in an air-raid warning, Grace miscarried at seven months, twins, a boy and a girl. Running, stumbling, from the bombs, she fell and lay bleeding half-way up a steep hill in London, panicked passers-by unable to save the lives of her new children. The ambulance came, finally, and took her with the wrapped bundles that were her unbreathing babies to the hospital. She almost died herself, wished she had, and lay for days with the futile tears streaming down her face. Ivy came in her off-duty hours and, grim in her tailored uniform, arranged for Grace to be taken to a rest-home in Devon, where she recovered gradually, painfully, alone.

Once, only, Ted allowed Ivy to bring the boys down to see their mother, but it upset them all too much; Ivy thought Grace might die of her sobbing when the boys went to see the grounds with a cheerful nurse. And little Tommy's angry shrieking when it was time to go left everyone white and appalled. Ivy could have kicked herself for not arranging someone else to take the boys back so that she could stay with Grace after they'd gone. She urged the nurse to give Grace a sedative, but she said she was still too weak, that they'd give her a wash and a cup of hot milk and put her to bed. Where Grace lay looking out the window at the smooth Devon fields, the low hills, the tidy hedges, the dirty clouds, and said, finally, goodbye to her sons. Anything else would have broken her.

Bill came back in time to fetch her home to London, where he cared for her thoughtfully and gently, cadged milk and eggs from his shipping contacts, stood in long patient queues for crusty brown bread or a piece of fish. They pooled their ration cards, and Ivy ate with them most evenings, sometimes bringing her lover, Fred, whom they all called the guvnor, and they would jolly Grace along, Fred flirting her almost back to her old vivacity. Ivy would persuade her to the piano and they would sing through the long blacked-out evenings, 'Lily Marlene', 'K-K-K-Katie', 'A Bicycle Built for Two', with Bill on his flute watching the forgetful pleasure on Grace's drawn, elegant face.

It was now that Bill began to talk to Grace about going to Australia when the war was over. He told her about the wide streets, the sunshine, the cornucopia of fruit and meat and fresh vegetables. Her Londoner's resolve to never leave the city began to melt – the familiar streets were becoming sinister; bad, painful memories in nearly all of them; the lumbering buses themselves full of pale ghosts, little boys in serge short pants, young tired-looking women with crying babies.

'Perhaps,' she would say tiredly, in bed at night. 'Perhaps.' And she would turn to him for his comfort. When he went back to his ship for what everyone was confident would be his last trip (the war really was just about finished), she was pregnant again, with her last child. Ivy promised to keep an eye on her, but Bill's absence dragged on. There was something wrong with the consignment, there were months to wait at the American end, he was trying to get another ship but everything was chaos. Grace became ill, kidney problems, and she was evacuated again, to a country hospital to rest for the long last weeks of her confinement. There was intermittent bleeding, terrible pain sometimes, and the baby was born prematurely, frail, needing to be washed in castor oil to protect her soft unfinished skin. Bill was still in New York when the telegram came: A daughter. Anne. Both well.

Grace took many weeks to recover from this birth; she had a lasting high temperature, still slowly bled, was put on tablets for her kidneys that made her restless and bloated and meant she had to give up any idea of breast-feeding. But she would pace, up and down the hospital corridors in the sleepless night with the baby over her shoulder, stroking, soothing, praying to any god that would listen that it would stop crying, would keep its food down, would begin to thrive.

When Bill came back she was already home in the flat. He was delighted with his daughter, but afraid to pick her up in those first months, she seemed so fragile. Bill cooked, changed the sheets, shopped, but Grace had no one to take the baby when the anxious weary tears ran. She sood at the window holding her grizzling burden, staring at the rubble, the half-demolished buildings across the road.

The old man, Clive, came sometimes to see his grandchild, and Olive too, on the train from Sussex, where she had spent the war with Lily and her family. Clive had done well out of the war, had bought up bombed blocks and was turning them into parking lots. He had grown plump too, with his black market friends, but his blue eyes could still glitter maliciously when he talked to Bill. He had never quite forgiven Bill's well-intentioned delivery of coal one winter that had buried his spare wooden arm in the cellar. He still lived with Letty Green, but spent many of his weekends in Sussex, where Lily grudgingly kept him a room in the boarding-house she ran with her husband.

Bill and Grace went to Sussex for a holiday and she gradually began to put on some weight and the hollows around her fine eyes began to smooth away. The baby thrived there too, with the long walks in her high pram across the meadows. Bill started to relax; then he became anxious to resolve what they were going to do.

They went to Brighton for a day on the bus, and he kicked scornfully at the pebbled beach, describing miles of white sand and surf rolling onto it of a blue no English person would believe. He looked at Grace, wrapped in the cashmere pullover he had brought her from America and her grey, well-cut flannel slacks.

'You only dress like that in winter at home,' he said. 'Not to come to the beach in spring.' His look took in the baby, too, swaddled and bonneted and he thought with a pang of his sons as babies, half naked for most of the year, brown and tough.

He kept telling her about his home as they walked along the peaceful overshadowed lanes, with pale primroses under all the hedges, and she looked around wearily at the ancient over-used countryside and knew that she could not live here, either. It was London – or somewhere else completely.

She joked about it, about being afraid of wild kangaroos and bushmen, but he could see in the end she was coming round. Now he became enthusiastic, began to let her see the detailed plans he had already worked out. They wouldn't even need an assisted passage – he could bring his family home for nothing. They'd go to Adelaide, Bill said, they could stay with his sisters until they found something. He gave up a quick thought of the boats again with little regret. There'd be jobs for trained engineers somewhere; yet he was already forty-eight, he must have known it mightn't be that easy. But as he talked the thought of the jacarandas blossoming, the purple heat of summer, overwhelmed him. He had been away for over six years, years of cold seas, near drownings, fear, and of his passion for Grace.

'Yes,' she said at last. 'All right. But not the bush with bloody wild animals everywhere. A city. A nice house somewhere outside a city.' She didn't entirely believe in Australian cities.

Bill took a photograph from the deck of the ship with his old pocket Brownie. Olive stoical in her black coat, Ivy laughing, waving, throwing streamers, Olivia trim and slightly disapproving in her air-force uniform, still working as an aide to some after-the-war official. When he had the print developed the sense of movement was almost visible, the small group on the quay seeming to be the ones receding.

4

Had the complaining started before they disembarked? I know that both their memories of landing at Fremantle were similar: the rain, the endless patient lines at customs, my mother almost in tears, 'But you promised me the sun would be shining. Bloody come to sunny Australia, you said.'

Then the coastal steamer to Adelaide, crowded, uncomfortable, and the suddenly excessive heat. Grace in terror perhaps, at what she had left, what she was coming to, how she would face his sisters, the friends of his ex-wife, respectable church-going bourgeois with grown-up families.

My memories of those aunts are recent. By then they and Grace had become friends, and I loved them when they came to visit us, or later when I was allowed to go to Adelaide alone to stay with them. Jolly, unconventional drinking women, theirs the easy laughter of the comfortable, not my mother's wry humour.

But in those first few months it can't have been easy. Grace, the new wife, their age but with a baby the same age as their grandchildren. Australian suburban living seemed primitive to Grace; outside dunnies and laundries with steaming coppers, dry grassless plots, heat and flies. She wept often, during the days when Bill was looking for work, at home alone with the baby and the unwieldy wet washing heavy on the old white axe-handle used to stir the copper. She sat in darkened rooms craving cool shade, pale, sweating, too listless to walk to the shops, which were miles away anyway. She nagged Bill: she had to get away, somewhere cooler, she hated Adelaide, his sisters looked down on her, she had to watch her language, they stared at her bright lipstick, they thought he had married beneath him.

Bill was never easy-going. He quarrelled with his sisters on Grace's behalf, a quarrel that took years to heal. A job came up in a paper mill in Victoria, but that was the countryside, she'd said she wanted a city. By then she didn't care, she was too eager to go, anywhere.

They drove, everything crammed into Bill's lovely old touring car, camping along the road, which I remember Grace always hated – the possums scrabbling on the car roof at night, the cows pushing threatening faces at the bars of nearby fences, the whining mosquitos.

When they reached Gippsland there were no facilities. The company was still in the process of building houses for its employees; meanwhile there were large tents and lurching caravans on bricks. We were given a caravan with a tent attachment because of me, the baby.

'Well,' Bill said, seeing Grace's dismay, 'we'll just have to make the best of it.'

Grace said nothing. But clearly in some ways she did make the best of it; the two years we spent there were woven often into her story-telling later. At least there were the other women.

I wonder if I really remember Ellie, or whether she is in my mind from Grace's telling of her. Enormously fat Ellie, who wore blue serge sacks and minded me when Grace worked at the canteen. She became Grace's best friend, and tears would still come to her eyes years later when she recalled the hard life that Ellie had and her boundless cheer and generosity.

'She never took money for minding you,' Grace would say. 'She always said her own little girl loved having you around, and she loved you herself like a daughter. Nothing was too much trouble for Ellie, even with her terrible legs and her heart, and her bloke belting her black and blue every pay-night.'

These must have been years when Bill and Grace might have built a lasting affectionate marriage. Grace had her three days at the canteen, Bill was busy helping set up the machinery for the new plant, there were frequent parties around the tents in summer or in the mess hall. Perhaps it was Grace's flirtatiousness, Bill's revealed asceticism. Perhaps it came down to class, in the end – Bill would have felt left out among all those shift-workers, and older too than most of them. He might have begun to play the flute again, preferring to sit alone with me in the caravan practising while Grace played the piano for the dancing.

And the women. Grace would have been at home among them, in that powerful female subculture with the babies, and the men at work and the gossip and marital revelations. They knew everything, the women, and the men hardly guessed. Bill might have felt she was slipping away, his precious prize, into a common-ality he barely understood. And for her he had perhaps become, with some relief, simply another husband, and slightly to be pitied for, at that, not having his beers after work with the others, seldom joining the parties, uninterested in bingo nights or the two-up schools.

'Do you have to go out every night?' He might have said to her.

'Well,' Grace looking at the crowded caravan, the wet baby clothes drying on a rack in the corner, the wireless turned to a discussion programme, 'I promised I'd play. Anyway, I won't be late.'

'At least you don't have to walk back with Taffy all the time. People will talk.'

'Oh? Don't be silly. People talk anyway, and we're on his way.' But making a mental reservation. She was, and would continue to be, frightened of Bill's anger. She wasn't stupid, had never intended to go beyond flirtation. She still clung to Bill at night, still stirred him to passionate gratitude.

'Why don't you come with me?' Softening towards his lean angry face. 'Come on. Ellie'll look in on the baby. They can put the gramophone on for a while, we haven't danced together for weeks.' Grace in beaded crepe, smil-ing, her hair unflatteringly permed, but still beautiful. (I have a photograph of her then. She had put on weight, her face was fuller, her body almost matronly, but her shadowed eyes, her full mouth, the creamy shoulders and deep inviting breasts set her apart still.)

He must have given in sometimes, then. Dancing with her, a waltz or a slow foxtrot, he would not mind the other men's glances. She was his and it was still all worthwhile.

I am sitting on a rug in long grass, with daisies. I have on a frilly white dress and a poke-bonnet; it is my first birthday. I squint, sepia-tinted, into the camera, and my eyes are shadowed, large and narrow, slighty down-turned, like Grace's eyes; I am an attractive baby and have already walked and talked for some months. I look smug, well-loved. Ellie has smocked the dress in pink, with rosebuds, tiny brownish splodges in the photo-graph. We have only been there a week or so but I am the youngest child at the camp and spoilt by everyone.

'Ellie really taught you to speak,' Grace said. 'You even knew a few words of Greek at one time. Oh,' she would sigh, 'she did beautiful needlework, Ellie did, with those huge fat hands of hers.' Then perhaps out would come the exquisitely crocheted dressing-table set of cream silk, Ellie's farewell gift. And I would hear again how Ellie loved me, and about Grace's sadness at not having kept in touch, the letters somehow dwin-dling to cards at Christmas, then to nothing at all.

It must have hurt Grace to leave, but Bill had been promised the management of a cool store and the big house that went with it. There were no prospects at the mill, the plant was in, all he could look forward to was shift maintenance work there. We needed to settle, I needed a proper house, a proper childhood in a big garden. But Grace had become used to the gypsy life, the communal laundries, the crowded outdoor socia-bility. She was happy there though she would grumble later, telling me about it – the days spent in rubber boots trudging through winter mud to clotheslines, the time the tent fell in under the heavy rain, the day she woke up to see a cow's head pushing through the flap and no one hearing her screams, so that she had to chase it away with a mop, as terrified as the animal.

5

Well, she couldn't help it, she would say to Annie often, years later. She just sat down and wept. The house was all right from the outside, a large white weatherboard, with attics; an acre of wild but once carefully planted garden, a deep stand of gums and undergrowth along the front road and the pine windbreak of an orchard across the lane. But it had been uninhabited for nearly a year and when they opened the back door the soot crumbled out to meet them.

'Knee deep, it was,' Grace would say. 'We'd been driving since dawn, you were grizzling. And *him*,' the lips pursed, well, of course, *him*, 'he had to go straight off and see about his work.'

But it was how she met Peggy. First the cackle of laughter, then, as she saw Grace's real distress, the offer to help.

'I saw you drive up and just wondered if you needed anything. I live across the road,' she gestured to a dense cypress hedge beyond the gums, and the outlines of buildings. 'I reckon we need a couple of shovels first off.'

Grace stood helplessly, holding her small daughter, while Peggy went back across the road and returned, hefting the two shovels under one arm. They worked well into the dusk, making a pile of soot and rubbish by the abandoned chicken shed, and Peggy brought her own youngest child, Hazel, to keep Anne company. Meanwhile the van arrived and Grace's carefully chosen hire purchase furniture had to be unloaded into the front room. When Bill came back from his drinks with his new bosses, the women had achieved a kind of order, and he found them cosy on packing cases drinking tea from a thermos in the black-streaked kitchen, while the children, ecstatic with unchecked dirtiness, ran about shrieking and laughing.

Bill disapproved of Peggy from the start – 'Common as dirt,' he would often say about her – but she was to become Gracie's solace in that first year. From then on there was seldom a day when the two women did not spend part of the morning together, drinking tea, while the toddlers became inseparable, running between the houses across the safe country road, nestling into the prickly undergrowth at the front of the house, wandering in Peggy's paddocks among the cows and the old carthorses. Peggy helped Grace whitewash the kitchen, showed her how to pickle eggs in a large speckled vat, gave her half a dozen of her own chicks to start with, lent her preserving jars, hemmed curtains.

If Grace was restless in this rural peace she didn't show it at first. She was still flattened by her life, still half believing it would all come to disaster again. She spent her days, when the domestic chores were done, and after she and Peggy had had their tea and their amiable, formless gossip, furiously working in the garden. She weeded for hours, and went to local bazaars with Peggy where she could buy cheap cuttings. She struck up acquaintances with other women there, and would sometimes put on her coat and scarf and take her shopping bag to their houses, where they would walk around the garden and Grace would cadge slips of anything that took her fancy. She didn't listen to the warnings – 'You'll never get daphne to grow in this soil from a cutting . . .' – and she was usually right. She discovered, thinning the nasturtiums in the square beds at the side of the house, the remains of herbaceous borders, and she cleared and planted them again, with pinks and violets to give them colour.

Gradually her English pale softness turned more sinewy and brown, and she began to look more like the other women of the district. Gradually she began to be accepted by the orchardists' wives, although they were always to think her a bit of a 'character' with her quick cockney exclamations, her make-up, the inevitable cigarette dangling from her red lips. This was easy for Grace, and she played up to it, exaggerating her 'cor blimeys', her blue anxious eyes crinkled often with laughter.

Bill settled to his new job with resignation if not with pleasure. He knew it was the last job he was likely to get and he was grateful for it at his age. But the other men found him aloof, and he did not make new friends easily, although, surprisingly, he got on well with Peggy's bellicose husband, Dave, and on weekends they would sometimes stand idly by the woodheap smoking and planning the small orchard Bill intended for an uncultivated strip of the garden. Grace disliked and slightly feared Dave; she knew from Peggy that he often got drunk and would then beat her and the children. But he could be charming when sober, with that wild, slightly terrifying Irish charm, and she managed an easy, flirtatious pleasantness with him. Still, she preferred not to go over to Peggy's when Dave's truck was in the yard.

Bill did not want Grace to work, he wanted her to look after the house and the little girl, so she began to make some extra money by taking in boarders, young teachers at the nearby one-roomed school. They became friends, of a sort, and after their year in the country town would usually send Christmas cards and the occasional letter to let Grace know how they were going, to announce their engagements, or the births of their children.

Bill and Grace settled for a few years into a fairly conventional marriage. They were seldom alone together – there were always the boarders, at the dinner table, or sitting around the radio in the evenings, and on weekends Bill would hitch his trailer to the car and work at clearing the block of land he had bought a few miles down the road, sometimes taking the two little girls with him. He would fell trees, or slash patches of the dense bush, then call the children from their chattering games around the tree stumps and boil a billy, giving them cups of sweet, milky tea that smelt faintly of eucalyptus smoke.

As a treat sometimes, if he did not have too much cut wood to take back, he would let Anne and Hazel ride on the trailer with the little fat black dog, and they would arrive home wind-blown and excited for their dinner. There were always animals in Annie's childhood. Bill, brought up on the farm, liked to have them around; Grace, with her easy kindness, found it impossible to refuse the little girl the puppy and the kittens and the pet lamb. There were usually five or six cats, and when some battered tom mysteriously disappeared, there would soon be a litter of kittens to choose a replacement from. Someone gave Bill a white cockatoo, which he built a large cage for, and then he acquired a parrot and some smaller birds. Most of the cats carried silver scars across their noses from their one attempt to get at the cockatoo.

Grace made some other friends: the dark, taciturn woman who lived nearby and who unexpectedly dropped in with her jams and preserved fruit, saying she had more than enough for herself, and Eve, the golden-haired young wife of the nearest orchardist. Kenneth, Eve's husband, became one of the two friends Bill was to make in that place. Dark and generally morose, Kenneth could reveal a sardonic wit and a sudden smile that Bill warmed to, reminded perhaps of some of the silent tough men he had worked with on the merchant ships. The two couples began to visit regularly, going on alternate Fridays to each other's houses, for a meal, and, when it was Grace's turn, for a sing-song around the piano.

Olivia wrote, too, that she and her new husband wanted to emigrate. Grace and Bill sponsored them for their assisted passage, and Grace waited excitedly for her younger sister to come. Bill arranged for them to rent a small cottage over the road from the cool store and Grace, with Peggy or sometimes Eve, cleaned it out and painted it and began to clear the garden.

Those early years in that house were peaceful, uneventful, I scarcely remember them as time passing, just a general sense of it always being spring; Hazel and I in our clean, ironed dresses and sandals, my little fat black dog at our heels. Hazel had a dog too, but her father insisted it was a working dog, not a pet, so that it stayed snarling at the end of a rope, a frightening obstacle to playing at her place. Dave was another – I was always afraid of him, with his fierce blue eyes and his black stubble, and the way he swung you up in the air and tickled you. Later, when I read endlessly the stories of Hans Christian Andersen or the Brothers Grimm, I found it easy to fit Dave's face to the trolls and ogres that gave me my nightmares.

I was vague as a child, my head always full of dreams and stories, often wandering off without thinking into some fantasy that seemed more real than life, only waking out of it when Grace or my father came upon me a mile or more away from home, their faces clouded with worry and anger. Grace told me often of the time I decided to visit my grandmother and she had, as she said, the whole bloody district out looking for me. 'Frightened me to bloody death, it did,' she would say, while I listened, enthralled, 'thinking of all the dams you might have fallen into. Then when you were found, after dark, under somebody's hedge, you asked if you were in England yet!'

Perhaps it was the very peacefulness of that life, at home with my mother muttering to herself in the garden, that led me to take so little notice of the things around me. Perhaps too, it was the endless, lulling conversation of the women, Grace and Peggy, woven around us from the kitchen as Hazel and I sat under the red-checked tent of our seldom-used dining-room table, playing our intricate games with my little peg dolls, or the kittens. That tapestry of muttered trivia and complaint, mutual support, exchanged gossip, recipes, that became continuous, picked up each day where it left off, sometimes going back to retrieve a stitch or two, repeat it in stronger colours, or to mute its previous stridency, often going off at seemingly irrelevant tangents, but always returning to the overall design. That absolutely essential, assuaging ritual of the way women talk together, the rhythms as repetitive and subtle as a Mozart piano concerto, and just as mysterious.

I don't remember the arrival of my aunt Olivia and Uncle Ralph, with Diana, my baby cousin. They seemed to have been there always, in the white house in the hollow over the road from where my father sat in his cold office and read his war novels, ate his packed lunches, checked the machinery twice a day or opened the storage chambers for orchardists coming with cases of apples or to take away their apples for market. So many of my early memories depend on the photographs in my father's later albums, and some of them surely were only stories woven around the pictures. So Diana at two, myself at four, sitting beneath a flowering fruit tree become the divine sisters I always wished to be one of, although in reality, I know, we squabbled and skirmished endlessly. There are many photos through the years of me and Diana, as if we did, really, grow together, yet Hazel and I were much closer, cruel to Diana when she followed us about, running away from her, teasing her to tears. But Diana and I are the couple enshrined in sticky corners: in matching pink frilled dresses sent from our grandfather Clive in England, in pressed pinafores with my pet lamb Primrose, or sitting tense, in the middle of some quarrel, on the low branch of a pine tree. Diana whom I never see now, whose eager friendship I so much regret.

And it must have been shortly after they arrived that it happened. *That which I can never try to remember, which sent me, you say, screaming out of the last hypnosis when you thought we were getting near. I remember the sobbing, I have told you that. Lying in my mother's bed, because I found it difficult to get to sleep in my own room (did they have separate bedrooms even then?). Oh, I remember the raised voices, the repetitive raised voices, and then I remember only my own hysterical weeping, louder and louder, why did they not come? Louder, screaming, banging with my head on the mahogany bed-end, screaming, screaming until finally they come, finally my mother sits with me and holds me and they exchange glances over my head and they stop their awful battering at each other and they concentrate on me, the five-year-old. I tear them away from each other. I make myself the centre, my mother is mine again.*

And shortly after that Grace and I went back to England. I don't know if it was intended as a separation, she always told me it was because she was homesick, her mother was ill, she wanted to see her family again. But we stayed away a year. We lived in London with my aunt Ivy, and then in Sussex with my aunt Lily and all my grown-up cousins. My cousin Terry, in his army uniform, teasing me, encouraging me to roller skate on icy pavements, my witch-like grandmother telling me the goblins would come for me after dark if I didn't eat my sprouts. Sundays toying with pumpkin and parsnip, aunts who didn't care about my fussy ways, putting the vegetables back into the oven when I went relief-stricken to Sunday school, the warm greasy plate ready for me when I got back, and no playtime until I finished the last retching mouthful. But my aunt Lily made me a strip of garden outside her fence, and helped me choose seed packets of colourful annuals, and watched with me while the fragile green shoots emerged in the chilly spring. And she sent me photos, for years, of my little garden, with its calendulas, its pansies and jonquils and white and purple alyssum. Why did I live in fear, then, of the whispered adult conversation, the nuances, where did that sense of dislocation come from? Did Grace neglect me in that year? Certainly I was often with my grandmother in the evenings, and my aunt Lily was the authority in the house. It was Lily who opened the side door to find me and the little girl next door with our knickers off exploring each other, who punished me with a spanking and kept me in after school for two weeks. Oh, the memories crowd now, that school which I attended in an anxious daze, not listening, hardly understanding the broad English voices, miserable for my mother and for Hazel my left-behind friend. Even for Diana. And the girl next door's mother had been in the Sunday papers, claiming her new baby was a virgin birth, a source of great muttered scandal in my aunt Lily's house. No wonder she watched us so carefully.

I sat outside the pub with pink lemonade, cold in my tweed coat and leggings, waiting for Grace, hearing her laughter, her warmth inside. I wandered in the meadows outside the township, stung with nettles, frightened of lumbering cows – was there really a ruined castle or fort there? Did I really pick creamy primroses in bunches I could hardly hold? Did my cousin Terry find me half-way up the dangerous steps of the fort or castle and carefully, patient with fear, get me down? Grace agreed, vaguely, when I reminded her later, was she listening? But she always listened. I was the one, later, who wouldn't talk, who retreated into contempt and irritation. Wasn't I?

Bill's letters, in the year Grace was away, were tender, persuasive. He missed her badly, he said, and Annie. Perhaps he was sly, too – he mentioned neighbouring women who brought him casseroles, dropped in with fruit and eggs. He told her how her garden was growing, that he'd picked two cases of gooseberries and that Peggy was going to make them into jam.

Olivia also wrote. She hinted that Grace should think carefully before she made the same mistake again. She said that Bill seemed very lonely. She had helped him re-paper the living-room, they had him to Sunday dinner every week; he had made Diana a swing.

Grace came home. She travelled on the same ship as the widowed New Zealander and his son whom she had met on the voyage to England. She played the piano in the ship's bar and wore a strapless black evening frock she had bought in London. The New Zealander, Wally, often told her she was the life of the party. Annie played with Robin, his son, and the children were put to bed in Grace's cabin while she and Wally went to the dances or the film nights or played housey in the salon. Annie half woke on these night when Grace came clumsily to her berth in the dark, and Wally carried Robin back to their cabin.

One morning Anne woke to see Grace slumped on the floor and she couldn't wake her. She cried out and pushed the bell again and again for the steward who couldn't open the door because of Grace pressing against it. Annie thought she was dead, but managed to half carry, half drag her to her bunk, letting the doctor in. Grace kept to her bed for a few days but was all right then. The word 'blackout' stayed with Annie frighteningly, and she reminded Grace often to take the oddly shaped white pills the doctor had given her.

Wally disembarked at Adelaide, he had relatives to see before he returned to Auckland, and Grace and Annie made the rest of the journey to Melbourne to find Bill, Olivia, Ralph and Diana waiting with streamers on the wharf. Bill seemed to Grace to have grown smaller, thinner, older, after Wally's red-faced boisterousness, but she never put into words what her hopes might have been there, and Bill accepted without comment the regular letters and photographs that came from New Zealand over the years. He did ask Annie once if they had seen Wally and Robin much in London, or Sussex, but her confused 'I don't know . . . Why, dad?' made him turn away, blushing.

Now Annie was at school, Grace said, she could get some work herself. She began picking apples for Eve and Kenneth, wearing men's dungaree overalls over her floral English blouses, her constant, humorous complaint at the weight of the apples in their thick leather bags, or the wasps, or the difficulty in getting up and down ladders, keeping Eve smiling, sometimes laughing helplessly, through the days, even Kenneth grinning at the sight of Grace perched on a ladder, cigarette dangling from her crimson lips, one hand with surprising dexterity snapping the ripe apples from their branches, the other gesticulating to underline her monologues.

She had never done heavy outdoor work, but she came to love it, the release of the full bag emptying into the cases, the tired pleasure of the cheese-and-pickle sandwiches and the thermos tea in the warm, rustling afternoons, the satisfaction at the sight of a tree bare of anything but leaves that had an hour ago been heavily laden with fruit. She became known as one of the fastest pickers, and later, packers in the district and Eve and Kenneth congratulated themselves that they had got her first, that the other orchardists had to wait for their season to be over for Grace to do a few weeks for them, enlivening their working days. Kenneth's orchard was convenient, too, in that it was near enough to home for the little girl to come after school, and Annie, with Eve's three children, was encouraged to fill a case or two of the sweet fruit and paid a few shillings. Or she would sit with Eve's fat white Persian cat in the packing shed, watching the apples tumble down the shute, and her mother, still with her long-ashed cigarette between her lips, lifting, swiftly wrapping in tissue, placing in arithmetic patterns the Granny Smiths, the Delicious, the perfect red Jonathons.

At home relations had somehow shifted. They no longer took in boarders and Grace had taken for herself the large, bow-windowed bedroom on the ground floor. There she had moved the mahogany suite, the Indian rug, the carved camphorwood chest, her crocheted dressing-table set, the ruched satin curtains. Bill stayed in the oddly shaped big room upstairs which he kept as neat and spartan as a sailor's cabin, the bed made each morning with a soldier's precision; a photograph of Grace, the twin to the one that sat on the piano, and one of Annie, on his bedside table, the picture of a schooner in full sail on his wall.

Annie's little bedroom was across the attic, and she was afraid to go upstairs alone to it each night. Bill went to bed early, leaving Grace reading or listening to the radio, and gradually it became a habit for him and the little girl to go up together, Annie allowed to read in his bed until she fell asleep when he would carry her across to her own room. When she was about ten he said this was no longer suitable, she would have to get used to going to bed by herself, and bought her a little night light to comfort her. By then the child's inconvenient presence in his bed had done its work – he and Grace no longer spent the night together, not even occasionally as they had sometimes done on evenings after he had put Annie into her bed and gone downstairs again hesitantly to Grace.

He became hectoring in those years, of Grace and the child. He criticised Grace's slovenly housekeeping, her smoking, her excessive drinking at their Friday night get-togethers, which now included Ralph and Olivia who had also become friends with Eve and Kenneth. Olivia did not work in the orchards, she didn't have to, she said complacently to Grace – Ralph had a commerce degree and a good job in the town – and she kept her comfortable cottage, which they had now bought and enlarged, spotless and tidy.

Bill had, while Grace was away, begun to clear his block in earnest – he planned to build them a house there, although the cool store had offered him the big white weatherboard very cheaply, and Grace would have preferred to stay with her lush garden. 'Still,' she would say to Peggy or Olivia, in Annie's hearing, and later to Annie herself, 'it keeps him out of the way.' Perhaps it kept Annie out of the way, too. Anne loved going with Hazel, and sometimes Diana, to the block, where they would be allowed to help dig the foundation holes, or be given slashers to hack the undergrowth encroaching already on the levelled base for the house. Sometimes she went by herself with Bill and she would wander around the five acres picking bunches of maidenhair fern, nattering to herself or to her little dog, or sit by the creek and gather frog-spawn in jars or catch tadpoles. Bill showed her how to trap yabbies too, with an old stocking of Grace's and a few pieces of bacon rind, but when she took them home Grace shuddered and refused to cook them. Bill shrugged his shoulders and threw the still wriggling things on the compost heap, where Grace complained about their smell for days.

The house would take years to build – Bill wanted this time to do everything himself, from the foundations up, and he only had the weekends to work. Grace was less than interested until the slope in front of where the house would be was cleared, then she came occasionally to start a garden and a few rows of fruit trees. Perhaps she believed, or she hoped, that the house would never be finished. The plan had only two bedrooms.

But she did reluctantly become interested in the garden, especially after the first year's planting began to flower and she realised how rich the red clay soil would be. Roses bloomed, huge, nearly black, their fragrance overpowering; bulbs shot and opened early, multiplying almost before her eyes; a patch of pale freesias beneath a small, budding lilac could make her catch her breath when she saw their somehow accidental beauty. And finally, she said, triumphant, she had planted hydrangea that did not always come up bloody sky blue. She began to spend at least one day a weekend there while Bill shovelled and concreted, watching anxiously to make sure the men in trucks delivering cement or gravel kept away from her flowers.

It is a photograph hand-tinted from my father's special colouring pencils: the tree is hung with tinsel and shiny balls from the cardboard box kept in the larder, at its drooping peak a star I made myself, cut out of cardboard and pasted with sequins and glitter dust. In front of the tree my uncle Ralph in a cotton-wool beard leans over to kiss Grace happy Christmas; in front of them (some of us must have been kneeling) are Diana, aged about ten, in a cotton frock with ribbons, her pale curls frizzed out over her shoulders; my aunt Olivia, prim and tightly permed; Eve, whom I also called auntie, her amber hair in a long, elegant pageboy; Kenneth smiling sheepishly; the Adelaide aunts, Alice and Mary, and their husbands; my adoptive godfather, Ewan, the handsome Scot who ran the cool store in the next township and had become my father's friend; Ewan's girlfriend Midge, blonded, with an anxious smile; Kenneth and Eve's children, I have almost forgotten their names – Tony, Rebecca, Fiona – and me, half turned to watch Grace, twisting a strand of hair in my fingers, not smiling. All crammed together like a human pyramid with Grace and Ralph and the tree at its apex.

I remember waiting for everyone to arrive that evening, sitting on the piano-stool in my best dress, picking out carols with one finger, hoping I wouldn't have to sing again, a duet with my father of 'White Christmas' which we did every year.

Grace came in, half dressed in her beaded black frock.

'Will you zip me up, Annie? Gawd, it's getting late – I haven't put any make-up on yet.'

I brushed my mother's hair aside gently and pulled

up the zipper slowly over the pale flesh, breathing in the scent of her talcum powder. She turned and gave me a perfunctory hug.

'Thanks, love. You look nice – come here, let me straighten your sash.'

I was sulky. I thought I was too old for dresses with ribbons round the waist, but Grace had for once insisted.

'Next year,' she had said, with a pleading smile, 'when you're twelve. You don't want to grow up too soon.'

She went back into her bedroom and I stood aimlessly near the window. I could hear my father in the bathroom, gargling his toothpaste and clattering things. I knew I would not escape the duet, he was already humming it. I had begun to answer him back by then, but I was still too afraid of his temper to say I wouldn't sing with him, or perhaps I still loved him enough not to want to hurt his feelings.

I wandered over to the tree and without touching them tried to read the labels on the small presents hung from the branches. I already knew I was going to get a bike the next day – I had seen my father carrying parcels into his workshed and he had come to dinner with paint stains on his hands. I was filled with impatience, I wished everyone would come – the Adelaide aunts were staying with Olivia – but there was that feeling, too, of wanting to keep the moment, the anticipation, of wanting everything to stay beautiful, unrevealed as it was then.

Grace, in her black dress, sat at the piano, vamping away at old music-hall songs of her youth. She was brought drink after drink – her Australian friends looked forward to this performance each year. Olivia leaned against the piano singing too, not as gaily as Grace, but you could see the songs made her nostalgic, softened the careful lines of her face.

Diana and I sang along, we knew all the words. I wished Grace wouldn't drink so quickly or laugh so loudly, but I was lost in admiration of her playing song after song, everything she was asked for, she only needed a few bars hummed and she could pick up the tune. I learned the piano, painfully, and could only play by careful reading. I longed for Grace's freedom.

Finally Ralph disappeared and we children looked at each other. Diana and I giggled. We knew he'd re-appear in the old red tablecloth with a red sock on his head and a hearty, if unsteady, 'Ho,Ho,Ho.'

The piano crashed to a final crescendo –

'Can't get away

To marry you today

My wife . . .

we all paused and waited to shout the punch line

Won't – let – me!'

The group around the piano collapsed into laughter and began a flurry of filling up glasses, wiping spectacles and finding a comfortable place to sit.

Grace stayed on the piano-stool, slewing it around so that she faced the room and her tight dress rucked up over her knees. I wanted to go over to her and tell her to pull it down, but I was too shy to cross the room in front of everybody. Somebody, our neighbour Ted Ellis, whom I didn't like very much because of his red face and sly nudging, had filled Grace's glass again, and her lipstick seemed smudged. But when I looked around the room I realised that all the adults were in some state of disarray. Eve was sitting on the arm of Ewan's chair, laughing, with her hand resting on his shoulder, and even Midge, usually so quiet, was giggling away quite loudly. Someone had been putting gin in her orange juice all night, and she had had to be dissuaded from doing a cancan. Ewan looked disapproving but my mother was nearly helpless with laughter. 'Fancy old Midge,' she kept saying. 'Fancy old Midge. Didn't know she had it in her.'

Dave came back and we had the ritual of the presents and the photographs, then Grace turned back to the piano and began playing carols. We kids settled on the couch with our games and lollies and some of the adults began to dance. I went over to Grace and stood by her shoulder while she played. Finally I whispered in her ear, 'Mum, don't drink any more.'

'What, love?' She smiled her wide vague smile at me.

'I said, don't have any more to drink. Please.'

Grace laughed, but she was annoyed. 'Don't be silly. You're as bad as your father. It's time you went to bed, I think.'

She went on playing and I turned and saw Bill looking for me.

'There you are.' He was beaming, he had had his Christmas shandies and someone had given him his annual bottle of cherry brandy. 'Come on pet, we'll sing our number now. Then I'm for bed.'

I was embarrassed and angry; everyone was quiet, fondly watching us as we sang, and as Bill kissed me wetly at the finish. I escaped quickly to the other kids when Bill said he was going to bed. I was determined to stay up this year.

I could see Grace's relief when he said good-night, and Ned Ellis moved to the piano and stood with his hand on her neck as she played the sentimental hit songs and old favourites to remind them all of absent friends. Olivia and Midge went to the kitchen to get the supper. This was usually when the children went to bed, after we had had our nuts and mince pies with whipped cream. Diana had a camp stretcher in my room and we both had our pillowcases set up there, with presents from our English relatives to be delivered into them during the night. Eve's kids went with cushions and blankets to Grace's bedroom. I whined to be allowed to stay up: 'Just this once. I'm not a kid any more, I'm nearly twelve.'

'All right,' Grace said with easy irritation, 'but don't make a nuisance of yourself.'

I settled myself with my plate of warm fruity pie on the old sofa in the dining-room, where I was out of the light but could still see what was happening in the other room through the opened double doors. Somebody turned the radio on and Christmas music interspersed with English comedy trickled through the party's talk and laughter. My aunt Alice came through and opened the door to the porch.

'It's too hot in here,' she called. 'Let's sit outside and see the new whatsit in.' She laughed, 'Oops. Wrong party.' She saw me watching her and winked. She was my favourite aunt. She went, singing under her breath out to the porch and peered up at the clear starry sky. Her handsome husband followed her out and they sat with their arms round each other, whispering, comfortable.

Ned Ellis walked to the door and asked what they were doing. When Grace came up beside him he put his arm over her shoulders then let his hand slide down her back to her behind. She said something to him in a low voice and he looked over his shoulder quickly then bent to kiss her, a long wet kiss, and his voice was husky and changed when it finished.

'Can you get out later, Gracie?' he said in the new. thick voice. 'When they've all gone?'

'I don't think so. Don't be silly.' Then she muttered something else quickly as Olivia came to turn on the dining-room light. Grace moved away from him and saw me sitting on the sofa clutching the old orange cat. Coming over to me she looked suddenly old and tired.

'Come on, love. I thought you were in bed.'

She took me upstairs and waited while I undressed and put on my clean white nightie. She kissed me good-night and went to the door. She turned and started to say something but I rolled over in bed away from her. I lay there when she had gone back to her party, in my narrow bed, the muffled sounds of laughter and music coming up the stairs, Diana asleep on the stretcher beside me, our empty pillowcases sagged against the bedrail. I switched out the light and watched the stars gradually emerge in the black spaces between the curtains. I turned over towards my snoring cousin and fell asleep.

6

Anne, as she grew older and went to high school, up late most nights with homework, woke every Saturday and Sunday morning to the sound of her parents' raised bitter voices. It was worse in the new house with its flimsy fibro walls, and she lay in bed in her lilac-painted room waiting, waiting with clenched hands for it to finish, for the slammed door that meant Bill going out to chop wood or clean out his aviary, that meant she could get up and make herself a cup of tea.

The arguments were always the same, they seemed to have no content. Grace would say something, perhaps deliberately below the range of Bill's bad hearing, he would say 'What?', she would repeat it in a high irritated voice, and whatever it was, however innocuous the remark, it would become a quarrel.

'It's time Annie got up,' Grace would mutter.

'What?'

'I said, "It's time Annie got up, she's got basketball today." ' Repeating it, Grace's voice would take on an edge, and Bill would use that as an excuse to rail against the girl's laziness.

'Well, she works hard all week, at school. Let her get her rest.'

'What?'

'I said, "She needs her rest!" '

'You're bloody two of a kind, you two. Lazy, untidy, look at the house. It's a brothel, magazines everywhere, dishes all over the sink.'

'Well, no wonder, in this little box of a place. There's nowhere to put anything.'

'What?'

'I said, "There aren't enough cupboards."'

'There's plenty of cupboards.' By now Bill would be shouting, following Grace about the small house as she worked, until she turned the vacuum cleaner on or ran water noisily into the sink, then he would pull on his boots and his overalls, his knitted cap, and stamp outside to his chores, or his beloved budgerigars.

Annie would get up, then, usually to find Grace still muttering at him her face twisted in anger, and she would hear the gist of it again, with Grace embroidering what had been said so that her own defiance had been stronger: 'So I told him if this bloody place was built properly we'd be able to put things away, and if he'd stop hanging his socks on the door, or get me a decent washing machine . . .'

Anne would sympathise, laughing at Grace's more absurd embellishments, save some of her expressions to tell her friend Ruth at school. At sixteen Annie still loved Grace simply, found her funny and brave, but she was also beginning to see the glamour of Grace's eccentricities, making, like Grace, stories out of the mundane trivia of home, telling Ruth fondly of the way Grace went to the orchards in four layers of clothing, her old brown coat over all of it, and her rubber boots, in mid-summer.

Ruth and Annie were romantic; they read George Eliot and D. H. Lawrence and wrote each other long letters almost daily in the school holidays. Ruth was going to be a painter, Anne was already acting and singing in local productions outside school. Grace did not like Ruth. She thought the friendship unhealthy, having read some of the letters; she thought the girls ought to be worrying about teachers' college, not all this nonsense about acting and painting. She said to Anne that she didn't understand half of what they were on about most of the time, and they probably didn't either.

But at home Annie was still Grace's ally. She had learned not to talk to Bill about anything important, and when she did speak to him her voice was sharp and loud like her mother's. When he had gone to bed in the evenings Annie would come out of her room and sit with Grace watching television, occasionally smoking one of her cigarettes, or having a small glass of beer while Grace drank Guinness. Grace complained constantly about Bill, how he kept her short of money, his habits, his snoring in the twin bed beside hers in the small bedroom. Annie had stopped urging Grace to leave him.

'I wouldn't give him the satisfaction,' Grace said. 'He can bloody support us, at least until you're working.'

Anne had also learned not to ask Grace about her other marriage, her other children. She still remembered Grace's collapsed face, her weeping, when, packing up to move from the old house, Anne had come across the box of documents, including Grace's divorce papers, and the little note written in faded pencil – 'Dear our mum, When are you coming home. We miss you. Love Tommy' – and its rows of scrawled and wavering x's.

Anne had been shocked, but excited too. 'Why didn't you tell me?' she had said. 'Were you ever going to tell me?' And Grace had said 'No. No. I didn't ever want to think about it. There's nothing to tell. It was another life.'

And Anne, intrigued by the separate lives of her

parents had wondered endlessly how they had kept it all from her, in their stories and yarns, how she had not noticed those missing years, those missing people.

Later, occasionally Grace made passing references to it, muttering that she'd have stayed with Ted, if she'd known then what she knew now. But she wouldn't be drawn to telling Anne what it had been like, how it had felt to leave her children, how she had met Bill even. What *must* it have been like? Anne thought often it must have been a great passion for them both to have left families, homes, settled lives. She could hardly believe it, seeing them together now, locked in their mutual resentment.

Anne had also found a flute, packing up, wrapped in fraying velvet in its leather case. Her mother had said, 'Oh, yes. *He* used to play a bit. I suppose we'd better not throw it out. You know what he's like.'

She had asked her father about it, and he had taken the instrument from her and played a few tentative notes. Then he put it back on its velvet, saying, 'I've lost the knack of it,' and she didn't see it again. She thought, later, that if she'd shown more interest he might have begun to play again, but she hadn't.

In her last year at high school, Anne played Kathleen in a production of *Riders to the Sea*. 'Bloody morbid,' Grace thought it, but the husband of one of Anne's teachers, who was a theatre producer, spoke to Anne later.

'They say I can board with them in town,' Anne told her parents. 'And I can work as a stage-hand at the theatre until I get some parts, and that'll pay for movement classes and everything.'

Bill and Grace were for once united in their refusal.

Acting was no sort of career, they said. She would go to teachers' college. Anne wept and raged, sulked for weeks, but they would not give in. Finally when her results were announced, she took a pale sort of revenge by accepting a place at the university on an Education Department scholarship. They didn't like that either, they thought universities were unsafe places, no one in either of their families had been to one. But they couldn't stop her, given the scholarship, and high school teaching was at least much more respectable than acting. But Anne had read enough English fiction to know that universities were also places of dramatic societies, and had been training grounds for many actors. She was determined that she would never teach.

Ruth had been accepted too, and she and Anne argued about her not going to art school. Their friendship had become obsessive in the last year, Ruth having decided that she was in love with Anne, and there were now manipulative games between them and a sort of ugly tension. Anne suspected that Ruth was going to university to spite her because she knew how much Anne relied on the old fantasies, Ruth the painter, Anne the actress. 'I can still paint,' Ruth said, but they both knew she was giving up on ever being more than an amateur.

Packing her things, ready to move into her university hall, Anne felt she was at least escaping. She was excited about university, thought of it as a place of social adventures, men, where she would do enough work to scrape through academically, where she would serve her apprenticeship as an actress. She couldn't wait to get out.

7

I was on my way to a rehearsal and was late for visiting hours. Bill had been in the hospital for a month this time, it was his longest stay. Usually they kept him there for a few days or a week after the treatments and sent him home by ambulance. He complained about the rough ride over the bumpy country roads.

I'd rung the hospital and they'd said they were sending him home the next day. At first I'd thought I wouldn't bother going in. I'd go home on the weekend to see him, then I remembered that Steve and I had a party we wanted to go to on Saturday night.

I hurried in through the glass door. An orderly was polishing the cold grey lino of the foyer, visitors trailed out of the wards. I breathlessly told the sister some lie about the car breaking down so they would let me in.

'Just for five minutes then,' the nurse said sternly. 'He's very tired tonight. I think he's been waiting for you to come.'

I crept into the ward he shared with two other old men. He lay quite still, his eyes half open. When he saw me he tried to sit up but I put my hand on his shoulder to stop him.

'I can't stay long,' I said. 'They said you weren't to be tired. You've got the journey home again tomorrow.'

He nodded wearily. His voice was faint now, he stopped frequently for painful shallow breaths.

'Are you coming home this weekend?'

'No.' I went on talking against his disappointed gesture, 'the car's got something wrong with it again – carburettor, I think they said.'

He closed his eyes. He didn't seem to care about the car any more, though when I'd first bought it he'd tinkered with it for hours when I came home, telling me what to look for, how to fix small things. He'd even made the trip to town a couple of times to work on it, braving the household of students I shared with Julian, sitting on the verandah to drink his tea, not willing to enter the messy, over-populated house. I'd put it down to disgust at my way of life, then, but now I wonder if it wasn't fear of what he might see – drugs, perhaps – or simply shyness in the face of the bearded young men, the women with their bizarre clothes and made-up eyes.

'There's money,' he said. 'In the drawers near my bed at home. A few hundred dollars. I was saving it for a trip again, but I won't need it now. Tell your mother.'

I didn't understand. Couldn't he tell her himself?

'No, I mean after . . . If . . . anything happens. She might need it to go on with.'

I wouldn't think of what that meant, but tears came into my eyes. The nurse came in and I bent to kiss him. He had closed his eyes again and I stood for a moment looking at him. There was nothing I could think of to say.

The phone call came early on Sunday morning. My eyes were gritty and hard to open, Steve and I had been up most of the night. He didn't stir as I pushed myself out of bed over him.

It was Olivia. 'Anne?' Her voice was distrustful, she knew the way I lived, and a male voice had answered the phone.

'I've got bad news, dear.' The 'dear' was an after-thought. 'Your father died early this morning. It was in his sleep, quite peacefully.' Then to my silence, 'It was better this way. He had a great deal of pain, you know.'

'Yes,' I said. 'I'll come down straight away. How's Grace?'

'She'll be glad to have you here. She's very upset.'

I went in and woke Steve. He put his arms around me, half asleep still, and I lay there for a while wondering what I felt. It occurred to me that the hospital had sent Bill home to die. Gradually I crept further into Steve's embrace and we made love, gently, and I cried a little.

'I'll drive you down,' he said, at last.

'Thank you. We'd better take your car too, I told him mine was in the garage.'

On the way, over those familiar country roads, I thought of the last time Steve had come home with me. It was months ago and he had only come because Bill was away. They got on very badly, Bill despising Steve's long hair and his actor's grace. Their only point of agreement had been politics, which surprised me. I had never realised what a socialist my father was, and it had occurred to me that there were other things we might have shared if we had ever learned to talk to each other. But I had been pleased that he wasn't going to be there and on the way Steve had joked about lying around in the sunshine, not having to help the old man with his chores, and us being able to sleep in the same bed instead of him on the couch and sneaking into the bathroom to fuck, furtively and quietly.

'He asked me to go with him, you know,' I had looked sideways to see Steve's reaction.

'You're joking! Imagine it – the old blowfly nagging and whingeing his way around the Snowy for two weeks. They'll probably abandon him and try to pass it off as an accident – "I'm sorry, miss, he wandered away, honest. . ."!'

We had both laughed, and I had stroked his fine dark face as he drove, loving the way he could switch voices and moods so quickly.

'We're here,' I had said, and sighed, as Steve let the car chug in second gear up the steep drive to the house. Grace's garden had been in full summer bloom, white apple blossom scattered on the lawn, rose bushes laden with heavy overblown flowers, canna lilies golden and red in a stand beside the drive. The garden was much too lush and elaborate for the little ramshackle house it surrounded.

Grace was waiting for us on the porch that day, as usual, the kettle was on, would have been on for the last hour, the silly big dog that we had got when my little black one died ran around us licking and leaping: it seemed strange not to see Bill straightening up from the woodheap, pulling off his mittens and cap to greet me. When we went in and sat down around the laminex table, I found Grace irritating, grumbling and gossiping, smoking cigarette after cigarette, littering the house with ash and red-stained butts.

She had clearly been revelling in Bill being away. Guinness bottles were stacked in full view by the sink, she left the lighting of the wood stove until the afternoon and we ate cold meat for lunch, not washing up until the water had heated in the evenings. I found myself annoyed by all of this too, though when Bill was there, lighting the fire as soon as he got up, the little house became like a furnace in summer.

Steve and I had lazed away the days, swimming, walking along the abandoned railway line through waving tunnels of mimosa and prickly scrub, reading or dozing in the old hammocks swinging between the tall sweet-scented gums near the creek, fucking at night in the narrow bed in my old room.

The night before Bill was due home and the day Steve went back to town for an audition, I sat in the garden watching Grace feed the hens, coaxing them into their run, blurred patches of brown and grey scattering in the dusk.

'How's dad been, anyway?' I asked. 'What happened about that chest thing? Was it bronchitis again?'

'I don't know.' Grace was dismissive. She sniffed, 'They say he's got to go back for some sort of radiation treatment or something. Starts this week I think.' She turned back to the hens. 'Get in there, you silly bugger. They're going to send an ambulance for him every week.'

I sat up. 'Why radiation? Isn't that what they do for cancer?' I looked carefully at my mother, noticing for the first time that she had become old. Her hair, dyed red now, was untidily permed, the rouge patchy on her soft wrinkling face. She stood still for a moment, then fumbled for a cigarette in her apron pocket.

'No,' she said. 'It couldn't be. They'd have told me, wouldn't they? No – I think they do that for a lot of things nowadays.'

I got up and went inside. I really didn't know much about it either.

When Bill got back the next day he had been full of yarns about his trip and descriptions of the mountains. I thought of the stories he used to tell me when I was little, and of his log books that I read, written in his elaborate old-fashioned script, catalogueing the arrivals and departures of his various ships, with occasional little vignettes, self-conscious but delicate descriptions of ports, anecdotes to remember when he got home. I found myself thinking that he could have been a writer.

On this bus trip he had been adopted by a young couple who had called him 'Pop'.

'It was "Pop" this, and "Pop" that. "Pop" do you want a cup of tea? "Pop" would you like to come for a walk?' he said with a reminiscent smile.

I had half realised, suddenly, that other people – outsiders – saw him differently, not as the ever-present old bully of my childhood, and for a second I tried to see him through the eyes of the young couple, a rather pathetic and lonely old man who needed a bit of jollying. It was uncomfortable, but I had told him impulsively, insincerely, that now I wished I had gone with him. He had seemed pleased, but in a vague sort of way, and later I thought he had already been drawing away from us.

Now, after his death, Steve dropped me at the house but wouldn't come in. I didn't blame him.

'It's a family thing,' he said. 'I'll book into the pub. Give us a ring when you know what's happening.'

No Grace on the porch, even the dog subdued, wagging his tail to see me but not leaping and nuzzling as he usually did. I found Grace inside, distraught, weeping uncontrollably, and Olivia on the phone to the doctor for some sedatives.

'Why didn't they tell me?' Grace said, her face

crumpled, ugly. 'They should have told me. I was going out to work and leaving him. I would have stayed home. They didn't tell me.'

I comforted her as well as I could, but I felt something of the same guilt and also blamed the hospital, thinking that if I'd known I would have come home for the weekend, bugger the party. Grace's crying made me tearful too, but I still could feel no real grief for Bill. *It was at the funeral, a few days later, that she broke. She'd refused to see the body, having a horror of his accusing blue eyes, but when she watched the coffin with its vulgar brass fittings being lowered on a sprung trap-door into the fire, the crying swept over her like a fit until she was shaking and retching, incoherent, and Steve had to take her home and give her some of Grace's tranquillisers. He sat by the bed, in her old room, stroking her arms while she wept and thrashed, murmuring to her, soothing when she sat bold upright and said, 'He didn't die in his sleep! He went to the toilet and mum found him there. She'd just got him back to bed when he died. He'd been trying to go to the toilet!'*

'Yes,' Steve said. 'Yes. Try to sleep, my love, try to sleep.'

'Steve,' she said, calmer, drowsy. 'Steven. Don't leave me. Don't ever leave me.'

I helped Grace pack up his things the next day. His seaman's uniform, stiff and empty on its wire hanger, his watch, his navy pullovers and old man's yellowing underwear. There was not much to pack. In a drawer was a box of ribbons and medals from the two wars – he'd refused to march in memorial parades; as an old man he'd come to detest war and all its vile subterfuge. When Steve had told him he was a draft dodger, Bill had said, surprisingly to me, that he would rather any son of his rotting in jail than fighting another of their filthy wars. There was so much we could have talked about, agreed on, if only we'd had time. In another drawer were his log books. I said to Grace, 'You should keep these. I remember reading some of them. There's some lovely stuff in them.'

She gave me a blank look, but put them aside. Years later, going through her things, I realised she must have burnt them. I asked if I could have his photograph albums, bound in Egyptian leather. I still have them; at least they were saved, with the little box of epaullettes and ribbons. In my will I have asked that it all be given to the Library – someone may be interested.

I also took his old soft leather jacket for Steve, though Bill would have hated that – his jacket, that had been through storms at sea, kept him warm in life-boats, going to the man he had no liking for. He had told Grace to disinherit me if I married Steve.

Anne met Steve at a party after the opening night of her first big part in a professional play. She was already living with Julian, had lived with him since university, and Steve had a girlfriend and a small child, but none of that mattered. It was immediate, magnetic, inevit-able. Anne had noticed him arrive – he was already quite well known – and she saw how people gathered around him. She stood on the edge of his group, watch-ing his clowning, his vital larger-than-life charm, his awareness of his own attractiveness. She always felt that off-stage, she was, if anything, slightly smaller than life. She waited until he noticed her and congratulated her on her performance.

'It was shit,' she said.

'Well, yes,' he said, 'But you were OK.'

They laughed, they were always laughing after that, then they danced and drank until the party was over and sat in his small car and wondered where they could go. Julian was sick that night and Steve's girlfriend was at home with the baby. In the end they drove drunkenly to his parents' beach house, where they fucked all night and most of the next day until Anne remembered she had a show that night and that she hadn't rung Julian.

After that they met as often as they could, in a loft that one of Steve's friends had abandoned as a studio – golden mornings and afternoons snatched from their daily life. Julian watched silently as she ran out of the house two hours earlier than she needed to, with some breathless lie about a run-through of changed lines, or at parties where she and Steve stood shoulder to shoulder in different groups, not speaking, or danced feet away from each other, averting their eyes to their partners, the line of tension between them surely visible. Anne was already angling for a part in Steve's next play, and at the audition was so full of determination and anxiety that she thought later it might have been the best performance she ever gave. It wasn't a major part but she was in nearly every scene, and her days now became crowded with Steve. They met at the loft in the early mornings, arrived at rehearsals trembling still with sexual excitement, rushed back to the mattress under the iron roof as soon as they finished. Everyone knew by then, but they didn't care. They saw themselves as golden, untouchable, until the day Sally arrived to pick Steve up, white-faced with what she would not admit, carrying the baby like an offering to her fear.

'Well?' Anne lay on the mattress naked after their frantic love-making.

Steve didn't turn, but stood under the rafters staring through the dirty windows at the misty city.

'She already knows,' Anne said. 'She just won't admit it. You've got to tell her.'

'I will.' His voice was impatient, worried. 'But not now, not while she's so insecure. I have to wait until she finds out about this job and gets the baby into a crèche, until things are more settled for her.'

'No,' Anne said. She knew how slippery he could be, it was part of his great charm. If things weren't decided now, she thought, while the passion ran so hot between them, she might lose him. She knew his kindness, too, and how he would miss his little girl, but she also guessed at his impatience with Sally's unhappiness, his wish to escape. She had already told Julian, had endured the days of his shocked face, his crying in the night from the other room. But she wasn't going to move out until she was sure of Steve.

'It's no good,' she said. 'I think we'd better not see each other until you've worked out what you really want to do.'

I was so confident in those days, so sure of his love and mine. He would often tell me that he adored me, lying beside me and stroking the hair away from my forehead with shaking fingers. I was so smug, watching people wondering what it was between us – I was so quiet often, but I knew that was what he liked, depended on, and I could make him laugh, always.

77

And he loved my body, lithe, smooth, the huge nip-
ples on my boy's flat breasts. We could never stop
touching, then, stroking, cupping, fingering . . .

'Be reasonable, Annie,' he said. 'How can we not
see each other? We've still got two weeks of the play
to run.'

She knew that, was counting on it. She knew he would
not be able to stand seeing her every night, not touching. She said nothing, watching him at the window, his
fine graceful actor's body, the line of dark hairs across
his shoulders, his underslung narrow buttocks.

His hands gripped the window-sill, then his shoulder slumped and she knew she had won.

'All right,' he said, 'I'll tell her tonight.' He stared
at Anne, 'I suppose we'd better find somewhere to live.'

He came over to the bed and I pulled him down to
me. Making love I felt that I drew everything of him
into me. I wanted to tell him that I would give him
everything, everything he had lost and more, but we
didn't speak. I thought that with time he would share
my exultation.

I have lost all the photographs from the wedding except
this one, but it is enough: Steve and I, arm in arm,
with Grace beside us, tipsy and slightly tearful; Aunt
Alice behind her, bemused – this has not been her idea
of a wedding, and she has come all the way from
Adelaide – and Olivia and Diana, equally disapproving, on the other side of Grace.

I wore a long blue dress of paisley chiffon, one red
rose in my floating hair, matching the one in the but-
tonhole of Steve's white suit. We are beautiful in this

photograph, both of us, though I could often look plain, with my small pale face, and my hair in some lights looked ginger. Steve with his sly dark eyes, his soft black hair; me surprisingly like a younger Grace, with the same slanted eyes, my hair a paler red but pretty. We are not smiling, we stare at the camera – Steve and I have smoked a lot of dope in the garden. I think that is Ruth in the background, turned away from the photographer. She came reluctantly to my wedding, after tearful scenes when I told her I was already pregnant, that we were moving interstate and didn't want to further upset Grace, who was so unexpectedly shaken by Bill's death.

'I will dance at your wedding,' Ruth said. 'I'll even give you a present. But I'll never forgive you. You will ruin your body with children and yourself with marriage. You know that.'

I'd shrugged it off – I thought Ruth was over-dramatising as usual. But we didn't see each other for years after that, and the heavy casserole she gave us was one of the first things broken.

Perhaps it was the house we lived in that first year we were in Sydney – dark, too big for us, with its overgrown, tangled garden sloping down to a cliff edge. Perhaps it was the pregnancy. *The nights when Steve was filming and she lay, queasy, lonely, suspecting ghosts in the unused rooms, aware of unhappiness hovering in the hallways, waiting for him to come home.* We didn't quarrel – we were always tender with each other – but we grew apart somehow, became . . . abstracted, in that time.

He was busy, this film role would almost certainly lead to others, and I had nothing to do but try not to vomit too often, and the minimal housework needed for two people, one of whom was seldom in except for breakfast and to sleep. I grew tired of preparing meals only to have Steve ring and say the shoot was going over time and he'd grab a hamburger on his way home. I began to live on dried fruit and nuts, salad, food that needed no preparation but was still good for the baby growing inside me. I slept a lot, or read, sitting outside in the garden. Every day I would force myself to walk for half an hour; sometimes I'd work desultorily in the garden, clearing patches of earth that I thought I might plant later with gardenia and daphne; aromatic, exotic flowers that would wave their scents at night under the camphor laurel. I did get as far as putting a frangipani in the small square plot at the front of the house, but we were not there long enough to see it flower.

As the pregnancy went on I stopped feeling sick and sometimes met Steve late at night at a restaurant, with his friends. His part in the film was over, he had a good role in a play, and he often ate with the other actors after the show. I felt I was changing – I had always been gregarious until then, loving the late night, adrenalin-flowing society of actors and theatre-goers, but these days I felt disconnected, and I put it down to being pregnant. There was a young woman, a journalist called Marie, who was often at these dinners, and one night she said to me, 'Steven's a very attractive man. Don't you ever feel jealous at all the attention he gets?'

I looked at him talking animatedly, basking in the admiration of people who had been to the play, showing off. He saw me watching and winked.

'No,' I said, laughing. 'He always comes home to

me.' Which he did, hurriedly, as if he thought I might not be there waiting, relieved and grateful when I woke and put my arms around him, drew him into our love-making, reverent now because of the baby. I glowed, I think, in those months; I felt we held each other inside a charmed circle, that nothing bad would ever happen to us, that we were touched by the gods. Well, I had read enough Greek tragedy to know what that meant, but I didn't believe it.

One night Grace rang, to tell me that her father had died. She was crying over the phone and it annoyed me – she had never spoken fondly of him.

'He went back to stay with gran when he knew he was dying,' she said. 'She was with him at the end.'

'Well,' I said, 'that must have been fun for everybody.' I thought of my vindictive grandmother, having him under her thumb at last.

Grace laughed, 'Yes. Still, he was nearly ninety. Poor old bugger.'

She said she would come up in time for the baby. I didn't want her to, but I could think of no way to stop it. Steve was pleased – he would be away most days, he thought I should have someone to look after me. He liked Grace, she didn't irritate him the way she did me, with her constant muttering, her refusal to look at what my life was really like, her harping on Diana's success as a teacher. He played up to her flirtatiousness with his actor's insincerity I thought. They both irritated me when they were together; I felt he diminished her, that she diminished herself with her elderly, rouged, coquettishness. I still had an ideal of my mother perhaps, thought she should have grown old with some dignity, some serenity. *And thinking*

*that, she refused to think that she was becoming like
her father. Bill haunted her in those sleepless weeks
when she could find no comfortable position for her
swollen body. She dreamt him alive in nightmares
where she had given birth to some furry creature, like
a cat, but with no face. He was there, at the birth, taking the swaddled bundle gently from her while she
waited anxiously to see if he would notice anything
wrong. She woke from those dreams sweating and crying out, but she could not tell Steve the details. He
would get up and make her a cup of hot milk, then
stroke her back until she fell asleep again. In the mornings after, she would shut their pretty little cat outside
all day and push her roughly off the bed in the
evenings.*

In the six months since I had seen her, Grace seemed
to have grown frail. She was vague, as usual, forgetting where she had left her cigarettes, her bag, the green
cough-drops she sucked all the time. She left trails of
used ashtrays and lolly wrappers through the house
that I had to pick up after her. The sitting-room was
littered with her paraphernalia – the uneven knitting
for the baby, her cardigans, her boxes of tissues, her
glasses, the women's magazines and books of cross-
word puzzles. I held my tongue, but sat outside more
and more in the sun, leaving her to the afternoon television in the dim, cluttered house. She seemed not
really strong enough to do the shopping, but she
insisted, and she prepared the vegetables for the meals
I cooked again in the evenings because she was there,
and because Steve was rehearsing a new play and was
home at night. Grace obstinately began the washing-
up straight after dinner, and I stopped protesting,

although it meant Steve taking a tea-towel and helping her while I sat on the couch wishing he would leave her to it, that we could have some time to ourselves to talk.

'She drives me mad,' I would say to him in bed. 'She never stops talking and chewing those horrible sweets.'

He thought I was hard on her, but he excused it because the baby was nearly due and the long hot days were exhausting me.

'She's lonely,' he would say. 'She's doing her best to be helpful.'

So I made some effort, sat reading by the open window while she smoked in front of the television, pretended interest in the details of Eve's or Olivia's or Peggy's lives. It seemed to me that Grace had grown petty – she complained that Olivia and Eve were as thick as thieves these days, didn't seem to have any time for her. Yet Eve took her shopping every week and Olivia had her to meals and seemed to do a lot of her housework. She resented that: 'She scrubbed out the bathroom. It was clean enough. She didn't have to do it, but it makes her feel superior.'

But when the baby came I was glad of her presence. I hadn't realised how frightening it would be when the pains began, how alone I would feel.

'It's like dying,' I said to Steve. Then, trying to make a joke of it, 'Or shitting. No one else can do it for you.'

He was calm, he'd been through this before, but it was in Grace's anxious eyes that I found some comfort. I thought of the babies she had had, of her miscarriage half-way up a steep hill in London with the bombs falling and no one able to help, more alone than I have ever been. I thought I saw those memories in her face while she made tea, fussed with my suit-case. I felt very close to her then.

When I brought the baby home she looked after us both, taking him when he cried, soothing him, walking him up and down the garden, tucking him into his pram for a walk to the park. She was my mother again in those weeks when my own exhausted tears ran. He was a difficult baby, colicky, needing to be fed every couple of hours, hardly over his last feed when he was hungry again. I was too anxious, too weak to love him properly. And I wanted a girl. I had joked about it to Steve, saying if it was a boy I would expose him on a mountainside. I had intended to call her Tania, after my gentle piano teacher, who had dabbed her eyes with a lace-edged handkerchief whenever it was clear I hadn't practised my scales, who had told me I might be a good pianist, if only I would apply myself, who supported her husband's failing sheep farm with her music students. *Anne avoided looking at the baby's wrinkled genitals when she changed him, rubbed oil hastily onto him. She had insisted on him being circumcised, even though it was no longer fashionable and Steve was opposed to it. She felt some satisfaction at the dot of bright blood in the nappy.*

'He doesn't really like me,' I said jokingly to Grace. 'He only ever quietens down when he hears your voice, or Steve's.'

I felt it was true. It was as if I was their daughter, Steve's and Grace's, that they made a circle around the baby, considerate of me but excluding me. I resented it, but it suited me, too. I did not want to be bound to this red-faced infant in his cot, always seeming to demand of me something that I was not able to give. When I developed a breast cyst and couldn't feed him any more, I was relieved. I began to look around for a nursery, to talk of going back to work. Grace was worried, it was one of the few times she voluntarily talked to me about her other life.

'My second little boy died because I had to go back to work and he was in a nursery,' she said. 'There was a pneumonia epidemic, and they didn't look after him properly.'

Tears came into my eyes at the pain in her face, but I said, 'Pneumonia isn't something you can have an epidemic of. It's a secondary condition.'

She sniffed, she knew she had outstayed her welcome. She said she might sell her house, go back to England for a while, see her mother before it was too late.

'That's a good idea,' I said. I wanted her off my mind. Steve and I were looking for a house to buy, something small and clean and light, something that would have room only for us.

8

Grace went home, and then a few months later to England. We met her at the airport on her way through and she cried at saying goodbye to the baby, whom

85

she called her little precious, to my annoyance. We moved to our prim terrace house with its paved yard, its tiled kitchen and whitewashed walls. There were no ghosts. I planted a garden, neat and contained, with jasmine climbing on trellises, small narrow-leaved eucalypts, orange blossom. I finally bought my gardenias, and set violets over all the unused earth. Everything was blue or white, and fragrant, designed for summer evenings outside. There was already an old gnarled white camellia in the front and I planted strawberries and herbs in the little round space under it, where they would be mulched by the juicy falling flowers.

I got a part in a television series, the baby was at a nursery, we had a woman come in once a week to do the heavy housework and the washing. For a while things seemed to fall into place, and we were happy. On weekends we went for drives in the country with the baby, to picnics in the gardens, or to visit new friends who also had young children. They were Steve's friends, really, I could not bring myself to be interested in these young women who talked endlessly about their babies, their domestic affairs. I lay on the grass with my hand on Steve's thigh, listening to his lovely resonant voice, wishing we were home together, the baby asleep; or I sat, drinking, in untidy kitchens, letting the other women's talk flow over me, my ear tuned always to what Steve and the men were saying in the garden or in another room. I watched the children crawling around the floor, making messes, and wished often to be free of it.

Steve began to spend more time with the baby than I did, picking him up on his way back from rehearsals, playing with him on Saturday or Sunday mornings while I slept. He seemed to have infinite patience, always ready to stop what he was doing and pick up the clamouring child. I seemed to have no energy, I was lethargic and listless all the time except when on the set or when we went to parties at night. I saw doctors who thought I might have an iron deficiency brought on by childbirth, but the tablets they gave me didn't seem to help much. I began to take speed again, as I had to get me through my exams at university, just to last the days, but it interfered with my sleeping and I often woke in the middle of the night crying for no reason. Once the crying started I could not stop, and it would go on for hours sometimes, into the early mornings. I would lie, shaking with suppressed sobs, trying not to wake Steve, resenting his helpless kindness, his questioning.

I grew to hate the television work, I wanted to get back to stage acting, so I auditioned for *Suddenly Last Summer* and got the part of Catherine, the most demanding role I'd had professionally. The speed wasn't enough, I started to use cocaine regularly to give me the buzz I needed for rehearsals. I kept from Steve the amount of coke I was doing, lying about how much my clothes cost to cover the money I was spending, telling him it was the pressure of the play that was making me so tense and irritable. I managed to get through the season somehow, even got creditable reviews, then I collapsed.

I lay in bed all day shivering and crying. I could not bear the baby near me, his noise seemed to drill right through my head, giving me headaches that lasted for days. Steve was not working then, he stayed at home and looked after me. He rang friends who said we could have their house at the coast for a couple of weeks.

'What about the baby?' I said. 'I need to get away from him as much as anything.'

'Well – do you want to go the beach by yourself? Get away from all of us?'

'No! No, I want you to come too!'

'Don't cry Annie, don't cry. We'll work something out.'

He didn't really like it, but he arranged for his mother to come up for a fortnight to mind the baby. I hardly knew her, but she was young and energetic, she said she'd be delighted to look after her grandson for a while. I knew she often had Steve's daughter to stay with her, that she probably still regarded Sally as her legitimate daughter-in-law, but I didn't care. I just wanted to get away.

We went to the beach and had probably the last really happy two weeks of our marriage. The house was a converted scout hall, on a rocky, coal-seamed headland. On one side of us was a natural lagoon, protected from the pounding ocean by a wide sand bank, and I lay here, on the safe island while Steve surfed on the other side. We went for long walks and found caves, where we fucked one afternoon in gritty pleasure, and then I picked wild daisies and banksia and put them in a jar on the rough-scrubbed table. We sat at night drinking gin and champagne, eating local oysters greedily, smoking dope and watching the possums and birds in the trees around the house. I fantasised about living at the beach always, but Steve was doubtful.

'I don't know,' he said. 'Not much theatre down here. And there aren't any schools for Nicky.'

'Oh,' I said, stretching out in the rattan lounge, 'let's pretend there's no such thing as acting. Or children.'

'But what would we do?'

'Just – have each other.' Looking at him there, in the moonlight, his strong face silvered, silhouetted against the dark sea, it seemed enough. We told each other we were falling in love all over again. I didn't want to go home.

When we got back there was a letter waiting from my aunt Ivy in London. Grace had had a stroke, a mild one, Ivy said, and she was convalescing at Lily's boarding-house in Sussex. As soon as she was well enough she wanted to come back to Australia. The letter was strained, formal, seemed to accuse me of neglect. It was true I hadn't written to Grace for some weeks, but her letters were sporadic too. At first they had been cheerful, she thought she might stay in England, she gave gossipy news about Ivy, now living with the guvnor at last, married, his wife having finally died, or about my cousins and their children; Coral, her wartime friend, home from America; Lily and her eccentric paying guests; my grandmother, bedridden now after being sacked from her charlady's job when they discovered she'd drunk their gin and filled the bottles up with water. But lately the letters had been different, complaining, querulous. She said that her sisters didn't seem to want her to stay, that Lily wouldn't let her help with the boarding-house and that she felt uncomfortable sitting around with nothing to do.

I rang Lily and she said, rather curtly, that Grace wanted to come home as soon as possible.

'She's really not very well,' Lily said. 'Will you be able to look after her?' The international line crackled with unspoken criticism and I wondered what

Grace's complaints about me had been.

'Yes, of course,' I said to Lily. And later I spoke to Steve about it, saying that I supposed Grace could have the spare room, that she could stay with us for a while until she was stronger. I had forgotten, I think, in my worry about her, how much she irritated me, and Steve was perfectly happy to have her.

'But won't it be a lot of work for you?' he said. 'Are you sure you're strong enough?'

I thought I was. I was off the drugs, except for speed very occasionally when I felt particularly tired or depressed, and I had decided not to work for a while. I slept a lot, or weeded my garden, and tried to take some interest in the baby, now speaking and walking, always wanting to name the pictures in his books. We had taken him out of the day-nursery for a few weeks after an encephalitis scare, and he and I spent pleasant days together, he was becoming good at amusing himself for long periods with his toys, and I was able to read while he bumbled about. Sometimes I would have an overwhelming urge to pick him up, squeeze his charming plump body to me, but he was an aloof child, waiting patiently until I was through, then disengaging himself to run after the cat or puzzle over his blocks. 'We respect each other's space,' I said to Steve, laughing, but I thought a little girl would have been more affectionate.

I didn't go out much, I got tired early and I knew I would be tempted to take coke to stay up talking all night with Steve and his friends. I was content enough, in a daze most of the time. I felt I was resting.

They brought Grace off the plane in a wheelchair, but apart from being a little unsteady on her legs, and her painful thinness, she had not been too altered by the stroke. One corner of her mouth was still slightly awry, though she said it would right itself in time. She had taken to half covering her lips with her hand when she spoke, to hide it, and I couldn't tell if it was this that made her speech indistinct. I did try to disguise my impatience at her mumbled complaints about her English relatives, but it made me tense with Steve and the baby. I was tense the whole time she was with us. Though I knew she found it hard to bend down from her chair to pick up her dropped bits and pieces, sometimes I had to almost run from the room to keep from shouting at her for her untidiness. The baby was more work with her there too. He remembered her and was always trying to climb into her lap, but she was not strong enough to hold him now, and I had to keep finding diversions for him. I thought that if I had to, I would keep looking after her, but I said to Steve that I thought it might drive me mad. *How can she explain about bathing that withered body, trying to avoid seeing the grizzled pubic hair, the wasted flesh, those skinny arms and legs and their hanging folds of unused skin? She concentrated instead on Grace's untidiness, her constant muttering, the familiar annoyances. She fought against feeling either pity or disgust, she repressed any expression of tenderness in case it burst out in a flood, uncontainable. How cold she must have seemed to Grace, how implacable.*

So I was deeply relieved when the letter came from Olivia saying they had got Grace a pensioner flat in the township, with paramedical household help. Grace had apparently written from England asking her to do this. I made feeble protests but Grace was adamant.

'You don't want me on your hands,' she said, her

unreliable mouth quivering. 'You've got your own life to live.' She told me about my grandmother and how she wore Lily down with her nursing.

'Well,' I said 'try it for a while, and if you can't cope you can always come back to us.' *Why couldn't she say 'You are my mother, I love you. It is my privilege to look after you'? Why wouldn't Grace say 'I am old and lonely and frightened, you are all I have'? Was she afraid to have put into words that she wasn't wanted? That Anne found her constant presence almost intolerable? There was nothing in Anne's rigid politeness to suggest otherwise.*

Before she left Steve and I helped her go through her papers to find her pension cards and local bank books. I sat on the polished floor of our living-room with cartons emptied all around us, and came across a familiar bundle in a large, crease-torn envelope. I put it aside, meaning to go through it later when Grace was asleep, but the envelope split and its contents fell out. I smoothed the top document: it was the certificate of Grace's marriage to Bill; the date was 1949 and the place Australia.

'Grace!' I was half laughing, remembering my father waiting up for me at sixteen while I fumbled with boys in parked cars after dances, his futile anger, his threats that if I 'got into trouble' I need never darken his door again. 'You and dad didn't get married until after I was born!'

For a moment her face puckered, then she saw me smiling.

'Well,' she was defensive, 'he couldn't get his divorce

through. Anyway, I'd changed my name to his by deed poll, so it was all right really.'

I looked at Steve, he was laughing too, and the baby joined in.

'Jesus,' I said. 'We needn't have got married at all. It was only because we thought you'd be upset at an illegitimate grandchild.'

'But it wasn't my fault,' Grace said. She was trying not to laugh as well, she didn't really see the joke. 'I would have been married properly if I could have. I couldn't help it that you were a love child.'

'Your mummy's a bastard,' I said to the baby. I was still laughing, but I didn't really know what I felt. *She was laughing, because it was funny, but there was resentment welling up, too, at the mealy-mouthed hypocrisy of the way she had been brought up, she felt she had been somehow tricked into marriage, into conformity.*

'Well, it's all water under the bridge now,' Grace said, giving in, clowning, but she was pained that we took it so lightly.

She left her things with us to bring down next time we drove to Melbourne. I have them still. Her divorce papers, her marriage certificate, the crumpled almost illegible note from her son, and a small grubby photograph that I only discovered recently, that must have escaped her attention all those years, of two belligerent little boys, squinting fiercely and clasping each other tightly by the hand. There is nothing written on the back of this picture as there invariably is on all the other photographs I have inherited, names and dates and places to seal the people and the time forever. The endless pictures of me – from an infant in a high pram wheeled by my grim grandmother; through my first day at high school, in my raw new uniform pushing my bike, with a kitten in the basket; to me and Steve and the baby. If she could see me now . . . *Yes, I know you will ask if that is why I am doing this to myself. I've thought of that, don't worry, but it doesn't seem to matter much.*

We flew down to have Christmas with her, and I thought I could stop worrying. She had acquired a boyfriend, a geriatric bikie who puttered up on his scooter almost every day to make her meals and took her in taxis to dances at the elderly citizens' club, or to lie in a chair at the beach. She had put on some weight and seemed to be less complaining; she basked in Gareth's attention and told malicious stories of other old ladies who flirted with him. He grinned with embarrassment and said, 'Now Grace. Now then, Gracie,' and to me, in an admiring voice, 'Your mother's a card. We have good fun, we do.' He brought her flowers, African violets in pots, and a green budgerigar that flew free in the little bedsitter, scattering the floor and furniture with crumbs and droppings, which Gareth cheerfully swept up.

They said they were thinking of getting the train up to Sydney, for a holiday, but that they would stay in a hotel. We made plans to take them sightseeing, to the Opera House, to the famous fish restaurants on the bay, and I thought it might be fun, with Gareth along, and his craggy, sly Welsh charm.

'It's obviously all she needed,' I said to Steve on the plane going back. 'A chap around the place.'

Anne was not with her mother when she died. They had been at the beach, Anne and Steve and the little boy, in a house they had rented for a few weeks at the end of summer. It had not been a very happy holiday – Anne thought that Steve was having an affair but she had not asked him. She had retreated into touchy silences and suspicion, privately condemning his unhappy questioning as fine acting. Now he and the child splashed in the shallows inside the sand-bar while Anne lay limp on the hot sand watching them, full of dark thoughts.

She heard her name being called and sat up to see the postmistress coming down through the thick pigface on the dunes. *I seldom remember things in colour, but that day is full of the neon pinks of the flowers, the postmistress's pale, green dress, the still, silky blue of the sea and sky, the brown of the man and the boy looking up from their game, the bright, bright yellow of the towel beside me.*

It was a telegram, from Olivia of course: Please ring. Grace very ill. Anne trudged back with the sympathetic woman while Steve calmed the angry child and collected their things. The silences in this phone conversation were from terror. Olivia was calming – Grace had had another stroke, she was in hospital.

'How . . .? How bad?' (Thinking, Oh no, not now. How can I be there, leaving Steve to do whatever he likes in Sydney?)

'She's in a coma,' Olivia said. Anne couldn't tell if she was crying. 'Oh, I don't know, Annie. Ring me tonight. I don't think there's any need to come straight away. When will you be back in Sydney? I'll let you know if there's any change.'

They packed up and drove back to the city so that

Anne could be near the airport. Then they waited for two days, ringing Olivia every morning and evening to be told things were no different.

'Go down,' Steve said. He was worried at Anne's strangeness – it wasn't only shock, she had been difficult before this, withdrawn. 'Go on. See for yourself. It won't do you any good fretting here.'

She was immediately suspicious. She thought he wanted her out of the way.

'What about the baby?' Steve was to start rehearsals for a play in a few days.

'I'll get someone to mind him. I can miss a few runthroughs if I have to.'

That was worse – if he could miss rehearsals for the baby, who else would he miss them for? But Olivia rang the next morning and said she thought Anne had better come.

'I'll just go for a few days,' she said. 'Unless . . . anything happens.' She wondered furiously if Steve's mother would come up, he wouldn't play around with her there, then she remembered she was in America. There was nothing she could do – she had to see Grace. She was being torn in half, she thought, between the two of them.

Olivia met her train at the country station and drove her to the hospital, hardly speaking. Anne didn't know what to expect. Now that she was here her head was full of thoughts of Steve and what he was doing. She met the doctor in the scrubbed corridor outside the ward.

'Is she dying?' If he says yes, she thought, gives me a straight answer, then I'll forget about Steve. It was a charm, of sorts.

But he was evasive: 'She's still in a coma. If we could get her to eat . . .'

'Aren't you feeding her intravenously? How can she eat in a coma?' Forgetting how much doctors hate knowledgeable relatives.

It wasn't a coma, then, exactly. As far as they could tell Grace was not asleep, but she was completely paralysed.

'You can sit with her for a while, if you like.' He was kind, but his stare disapproved of her smart clothes, her expensively cut hair, while her mother lay dying. 'Perhaps you can get her to eat something. She might even recognise you – sometimes we're surprised with these cases.'

Anne went into the room and found Gareth sitting by the bed holding her mother's hand, tears running down his seamed brown face. He got up when she came in and she took his place, controlling her shock at the fragile body that hardly disturbed the line of the too-neat bedclothes. She sat with her for the rest of that day, and most of the next, trying to push hospital pap on a plastic spoon through the slack lips every time the light, familiar blue eyes opened. She murmured to her encouragingly, as if to a recalcitrant baby – 'You must eat, Grace . . . mum, please. Just swallow. Just this spoonful . . .' trying not to bruise the gums with the shaking spoon (they had taken out her dentures). But apart from the flickering eyes there was no response.

'She's dying of starvation as much as anything,' Anne said angrily to Olivia before going exhaustedly to the chill spare room whose windows looked out across the cool store dam to Bill's old office. 'Why haven't they got her on a drip?' *Thinking Olivia unsympathetic, not realising that they were letting her die, that it was the lesser cruelty.*

'She was in the middle of making a cup of tea,' Gareth said, somehow blaming himself. 'She was just bringing my cup over when she seemed to shake, all down her body, and then she fell.'

'At least you were there,' Anne said, meaning to comfort, thinking of all the Sunday newspaper stories of old people's bodies, hands stretched out to phones uselessly off the hook, not found for days.

Then on the third day she rang home several times and Steve was not there. She had stopped trying to get Grace to eat, she sat with her all day holding the inert hand, stroking her arm, muttering promises, when Gareth was out of the room, that when Grace was well she would come and live with them, that Anne would look after her from now on. *But still, still the words would not come. I was refusing to believe that she would die, and I could not tell whether she heard me or not. It wasn't until I was leaving, frantic with jealousy about Steve, telling Olivia that I had to get back, that the baby was ill and we had no one to mind him, that I bent and whispered to Grace that I loved her, would always love her. I backed from the room, still soothing her, but when I said goodbye her terrible body convulsed under the blankets, her eyes widening into madness. It was too late then, I was going. But she knew me. She had been listening all the time. She knew I was leaving her alone to die.*

9

The day I left Steve followed me about as I picked up the last boxes and carried them to the car, still insisting that I had made it all up, that he had not been fucking Marie. But I blamed him anyway. *It was because of him that I spoke to you first, because he couldn't bear the accusations, the storms of crying that swept over me every night. And you believed him too. That's why I agreed to come here, that first time, that and your worried look when I told you I was more and more thinking of myself in the third person, as if there was no 'I', as if everything had happened to someone else. You had fancy terms for it then, you are running out of them these days. You are starting to believe me, I think, as you watch me disappear.*

But I did need the rest, and I met Danny here, which was nice. For a while. Early mornings, early nights, volley-ball three times a week, regular meals. I felt a lot better by the time I signed myself out, with Danny. I laughed at your anger that I had not 'responded' to therapy, your technician's wish that I would let you put electrodes into my brain.

I felt like laughing at Steve, too, at his dismay when I told him.

'You can't live with Danny,' he said. 'I'm thinking of you, too. For christ's sake, Annie, he's an addict. You don't want that sort of life.' He had not liked Danny when he met him on his frequent visits to me here, had watched our closeness suspiciously, had turned away helplessly when I told him it was sauce for the goose.

'But I do,' I said, and I did. It was fun for a while, too, until I got sick. And you have to admit that at least I never got onto the hard stuff myself. But Danny disgusted her in the end, as his body became emaciated again, and he would do nothing but lie in bed all day, the used coffee cups growing mould in a circle around the room, his kit in a little basin on the floor beside him. When she was first sick she might have gone back to Steve, but he was already with Marie. You say I pushed him into that, that by insisting I made it so. But I see the doubt on your face sometimes now. They are so disgustingly happy together, aren't they? And she's pregnant, so my child will have another sister. I do read his letters, even if I won't see him. Or brother. But I think Marie will have a girl.

When she moved out from Danny's sordid flat she had thought she would pull herself together. She planned the shape her new life would have in the bright studio with its tiny sky-blue bedroom for the child, who would come to her for weekends. She thought she would put up friezes and mobiles for him, that she would be more disciplined. She would use the weeks to prepare for going back to work. She'd go to movement classes again and voice training, she had become lazy.

But it didn't quite work out like that. The child was difficult, he clung to Steve's hand on Friday evenings, spent most of Sunday asking 'Where's Steve? Is he late?' When he left she would crawl back into bed with a drink and a handful of aspirin. The studio became messy, but she never seemed to have the time to clean it. The daffodils in the brown slab pot wilted and turned slimy, scripts littered the table, she told her agent she didn't like any of them, she couldn't be bothered auditioning. She spent the winter crouched over the heater, chain-smoking, drinking, spending more and more of the money Grace had left her on cocaine. But it wasn't the coke that made her sick, it was that she hardly slept, and she could never remember to eat every day. She told Steve she was too ill to have the child, and she wouldn't let him in when he tried to visit. One day she stood by the window face to face with him and the anxious boy pressing his nose to the glass. She could hardly remember who they were, although she spent much of her time in imaginary dialogue with Steve, consoling him, promising that it would all be all right in the end. But that was a different Steve, one who did not stay out late or fuck around, or reproach her for neglecting the child. A Steve who understood that I had Grace living on in my brain like a maggot, that she had been there since the moment of her death, that morning after Anne had got back from Melbourne, exhausted, after she had finally confronted Steve about Marie, brushing aside his denials. They had argued all night, their shouting waking the baby so that Steve went in to sleep in his room with him and I lay alone, falling into a deep sleep, waking an hour later already sitting up, saying out loud, 'She's dead. My mother's dead.' The telegram didn't come until lunchtime, but I had already told Steve she had died at four-thirty a.m. Steve didn't believe in the occult (I always have, since Ruth and I used to play frighteningly with ouija boards and pendulums at school), but that did happen, and Grace is still alive somewhere inside my head. She has got into

*me and she can't escape. You tell me that I did not mean
to kill myself, but I did. When I gashed my wrists I
was trying to release her too. Now I will bury her in
flesh with me. Or I will let you try your electrodes,
burn out my synapses – there are many ways of dying,
if this one proves too slow.*

Anne often sits in the courtyard here, which no one
else seems to come to – perhaps her presence repels
them. It has become her place, in a way, she has per-
suaded the gardener to bring in large pots and has
planted them with flowers she buys at the markets on
the days we are allowed to go shopping. There is even
a cat, an old fat tabby, that often joins her, though
he won't sit on her lap. She likes to sit and go through
the old photograph albums and the loose packets of
snaps that have never been pasted up. She thinks,
sometimes, that she should buy new albums and
arrange them properly, but somehow she never gets
around to it. This morning she had to sit in under the
eaves because it was wet, watching the rain staining
the azaleas. She was upset that it might completely spoil
the white one; that bush has been such a joy, gleaming from its dark corner. She looked at the cat
sheltering under it and made kissing noises to entice
him, but he pretended not to hear. 'Bad cat,' she said
to him; she felt uneasy this morning, she wanted to
hold the cat, feel it purring against her. When she heard
the familiar voice approaching she thought it must have
been a premonition.

Ruth came to see me today. When she opened the door

to the courtyard my annoyance at being interrupted turned to a quick leap of pleasure, like seeing a lover after a long absence.

I took her straight up to my room. I was excited. I made coffee and noticed her surprise at the little self-contained unit. Did she expect me to be in a strait-jacket, or sharing a dormitory of lunatics? She sat down by the window, she was hardly changed at all, still dark and soft, dressed with conservative elegance.

She was nervous with me looking at her. She fiddled with her keys, looked around the room, sighed.

'Steve's paying,' I said. 'He can afford it.' *Don't think Anne hasn't noticed the videos downstairs of some of his early movies.*

She gave me a quick look, then went back to staring at the distant hills.

'Why have you come? After all this time?'

She was surprised. 'I thought you wanted me to. I thought . . .'

I understood – you, interfering.

'No,' I said. 'I didn't want you here.' I still have the power to hurt her, I thought, watching her face, but she sighed again and turned to the window. She was clearly determined to see it through.

I went to stand beside her and for a while we both looked out. The rain had stopped, the gardens were glistening, dripping, I could imagine how the clean earth must smell. Finally we faced one another.

'You look well,' I said.

'Thank you.' She didn't return the compliment. It occurred to me then how much my appearance must have shocked her. When we were young, when she was going to be a painter, she was always telling me about my elegant shoulders, the jut of my wrists. She would hate my new body, which I like, with its hummocks of flesh and soft chins and comfortable rolls of fat around the thighs. Eating is such a pleasure to me now, stuffing myself full of cakes and chocolate and potatoes and rice. Caterpillars must feel like this in their cocoons, peacefully wrapping themselves in layer after layer.

She picked up her bag, she hadn't drunk her coffee.

'Don't go yet,' I said. 'Now that you're here. Come for a walk outside.'

I noticed she brought her coat, she was not coming back to my room.

We walked slowly under the wet trees to the edge of the old orchard and sat on the damp stone wall looking down the valley to the purple mountains. I could feel her looking at me while I stared at the shadows of the hills. They reminded me of something.

'Do you remember the holiday we had together the summer before we started university?' I wanted her to soften into reminiscence too. 'That terrible chalet in the Dandenongs and the carpet bowls and that old man who kept asking you to go away with him? Wasn't it lovely?' I had almost forgotten she was there, I am so used to my imaginary conversations. 'The river, and the ghost gums shedding their skins. The little bridge where we saw the wombat?'

I couldn't understand the tension of her stare.

'Do you really remember it like that?' Her voice was low and hostile. 'All shining and innocent?'

'Yes,' I was surprised. 'Though I suppose we weren't at all innocent in fact.'

'Do you know how I remember that holiday?'

'No. How?' I could feel a headache beginning.

'It was one of the worst times of my life,' she said,

104

looking through her cigarette smoke at the pale paddocks of the foothills. 'All I could think of was that I'd lose you forever once the summer finished. On those walks along the river, I was watching you, listening to all your plans for us – how we'd share a flat, and keep cats, be great. And all the time I knew that your grace and your beauty were slipping away from me, that I'd lose you to the first good-looking man who came along.'

'But I meant it. I never understood why you decided to go into college instead.'

'Yes,' she was thoughtful. 'I suppose you did mean it in a way. You wanted to have me with you, but you had no idea what it would do to me, or you didn't care. It was a game to you – a play you were starring in at the time. You never understood that I really loved you, it spoiled your scenario.'

'No! I couldn't cope with your intensity, it frightened me. I did want you with me, that's true, but I did love you too, in my own way.'

She went on as if she hadn't heard me. 'I spent those nights in an agony of frustration for you in the next bed. It took me years to realise you were probably frigid as well as everything else.'

I could feel the flush starting on my face, the headache was getting worse and my pills were back in the room.

'I'm sorry,' I must have been gasping, she looked alarmed. 'I didn't know . . . that you hated me. I probably did ask to see you, but I shouldn't have. I'm sorry.' Anne was starting to panic, she could feel the headache rising, rising. She wanted to get away from Ruth, back to her room, somewhere safe to wait for the rest of the pain, but Ruth wouldn't stop.

'You were always sorry after you'd ripped my guts out. I remember you telling me about a puppy you'd once had that you used to beat with a stick until he whimpered and rolled on the ground, then you'd pick him up and cuddle him until he licked you in gratitude.'

'Ruth! Please!' Anne couldn't believe what was happening.

'No, you asked to see me, I've come a long way, now you can hear it all. Oh, I know you probably thought that all these years I've been nursing my passion for you, for when you needed me again, but I haven't Anne. I grew out of it, the way you used to tell me I would.' She leaned towards me. 'I remember your pose at school – that you thought you were incapable of loving anybody. God knows where you got that from, some shitty historical romance probably. It was supposed to be your fatal flaw, I think, to set you apart. But it's true. Either you were right about yourself for once or you've simply managed to grow into the part. You've never loved anybody – not your mother, who you used to make fun of, not me, not Steve. Not even your own child . . .' She stopped.

'I'm sorry, I shouldn't have said that.'

'No, you shouldn't.' My head was bursting. 'You shouldn't have said any of it.' I had to get rid of her. 'You've given me a headache. It's not your fault, they should have realised I'd got it all wrong.'

I was trembling with pain and anger. She put out her hand to help me up but I moved away. She followed me as far as entrance to the car-park, then I walked on, but at the door I turned and watched her. Her face was white, it seemed she was crying, but it might have been the drizzle starting again. She sat for a while with her hands tight on the steering-wheel before she drove off. As she stopped to make the turn out of the drive she looked back and we stared at each other. She gave a quick shake of her head and accelerated into the road.

You don't believe that happened either, do you? Then why did Anne have such a terrible migraine when she hadn't had one for weeks? Not even after the last treatment. I can't explain how she got back to the courtyard, how you found her sitting there almost fainting with pain. If I was talking, it was to the cat that sometimes sits there with me. You think you will use this to get me to sign the forms again, but she intended to do that anyway, she wants you to burn out her brain. There is no need for her to make up a Ruth to tell her these things. Why not a Grace? Or a Bill? Or, since they're dead, why not a Steve? You know I sometimes have imagined conversations with them, why should I not report the terrible things they say to me? You tell me that I obscure everything, make up stories to hide the truth, but how many times do I have to tell you that Anne's memory is faulty, that she was always vague, even as a child, living in a fantasy world that seemed more real than her life? She has tried to tell you the truth, but you want reasons, and there is only what happened, what it was like . . .

My mother's name was Grace; she was graceful. She grew up in a slum in London and her father beat her with his wooden arm.

107

When I was little, she was warm and held me often; later she became complaining, complicit and hesitant. Her favourite times were in her garden, the cat on a fence-post somewhere near. She wore rouge in pink round spots, she chain-smoked menthol cigarettes and swore. She laughed with her mouth wide open – sometimes you could see the dentures – but even in old age she was pretty.

I loved her, my vulgar, laughing mother; I blamed her for everything. My memories of my father are soured by her muttering vindictive presence.

She lived alone, not intruding on Anne's married life. She would not say to her 'I am old and frightened, you are all I have.' Anne was her last, her only child. Anne was not with her when she died.

Anne was not with her when she died, her body convulsed under too-neat bedclothes, her eyes widening to madness. She knew Anne, she knew she was being left alone to die.

Anne loved her and she was not with her when she died.

Her mother's name was Grace . . .

Also published by Penguin

Country Girl Again
Jean Bedford

'Usually he climbed through the rough orchard just after lunch and came to her back door red in the face and breathing hard.

Today he was late . . .

She sat down at her table, powdered and painted, black hair carefully brushed, her red nails tapping at the laminex. She looked at her watch, fiddled with her tight brassiere, lit a cigarette. Well, he was late again. Different when we first started, she thought sourly, couldn't wait to get here then.'

Jean Bedford has a considerable talent for taking us beneath the surface of the everyday appearances and bold fronts women construct for themselves. She writes of women trapped, women ostracized, women on the edge of madness, women alone with their guilt and aimlessness and fear – but always she writes with warmth and a lovely simplicity that echoes on in the mind for a long time.

Beachmasters
Thea Astley

The central government in Trinitas can't control the outer island. But then neither can the British and French Masters.

The natives of Kristi, supported and abetted by some of the *hapkas* and *colons* of two nationalities, make a grab for independence from the rest of their Pacific island group. On their tiny island, where blood and tradition are as mixed as loyalties and interests, their revolution is short-lived. Yet it swallows the lives of a number of inhabitants – from the old-time planters Salway and Duchard, to the opportunist Bonser, and the once mighty *yeremanu*, Tommy Narota himself.

Salway's grandson Gavi unwittingly gets caught up in Bonser's plans and, in a test of identity too risky for one so young, forfeits his own peace.